Foreword

This story geographically wanders across various parts of
the US, between cities, towns and wilderness. For the most part, it is
based in the Dark Peak area of the UK's Peak District National Park.

The Peak District is a wonderful part of the country, characterised by
heather clad moors, gritstone crags, limestone gorges and strangely
shaped rock formations which sit upon tors and mountains. The high
mountain plateau of Kinder Scout has its own microclimate and the
unfamiliar can be caught out by abrupt changes in the weather. In a
matter of a few minutes, a sunny blue skied day can be transformed
into a dark, foreboding world of low cloud, hail and thunder.

Deep, moss-covered ravines known as cloughs, offer challenging rocky
scrambles up to Kinder Scout's wild and wind-blown summit. The best
known of these routes can become busy in summer, however I have
climbed the more remote cloughs many times without seeing another
soul.

In addition to its amazing scenery, moody weather and fascinating
wildlife, The Dark Peak area is renowned for its myths, legends and
ghosts, some of which crop up in my story.

Don't dismiss the myths and ghosts too readily. I have experienced
some of these first-hand. On one occasion I was camping with my
young son in a quiet field in the Vale of Edale. We weren't allowed any
sleep at all. The whole night we were kept awake by heavy footsteps
closely circling our tent. Every time I investigated, the noisy pacing
ceased and there was nothing in sight. The footsteps were too heavy
for a small animal and there was no livestock in the field. Needless to
say, my mind was entertained the whole night by thoughts of Owd
Schuck and The Boggart, huge black ghost-dogs that are said to haunt
the area. I later discovered that we weren't the first campers to be
haunted in that valley.

I hope this book evokes a real sense of place in readers and inspires appreciation of our country's amazing wild places.

CHAPTER 1

The Awakening

A warm night late in May 2019:

Disturbed from deep REM sleep, Drew felt a warm, sticky wetness on the left side of his face. Half wakened, thinking the room must be too hot and that he had been sweating, he wiped his cheek with the back of his hand. The dense stickiness and unmistakable metallic aroma of blood dragged him from the depths of his dreams.

As Drew sat up, he was hit by a searing pain on his scalp and he felt the warm trickle of blood tracking down his cheek onto his neck.

His heart pounding in his chest and sweat beginning to bead on his brow, Drew's eyes adjusted to the dim half-light of his bedroom. A looming shadow came into focus at the foot of his bed. This was some bad dream. As his vision sharpened, the shadow slowly took the form of a pig. A pig standing well over six feet tall. Horror-struck, Drew bolted upright and reached for the bedside lamp. Lit by the light from the lamp, Drew saw that the pig was holding a machete in its human right hand.

The pig spoke from behind its grotesque mask: "It's been a while Drew."

On hearing the heavy Dutch accent, Drew immediately realised what this hellish intruder was. He also knew the purpose of its visit.

The chain of events leading to up to this bizarre, nocturnal intrusion, had been set in motion almost a year ago, by a tongue-in-cheek discussion between a group of four mates in their never-ending search for new ways to entertain themselves.

CHAPTER 2

The Wednesday Club

At the age of forty-seven James Hurst managed to beat his target of retiring from the grind of the hamster wheel by the age of fifty. He had achieved this by a combination of right-place, right-time luck and hard graft. Over the past fifteen years he had built up an engineering consultancy specialising in the design of power generation systems which efficiently produce energy from plastic waste, while emitting the absolute minimum of pollutants.

James had timed his entry into the market impeccably, quickly attaining a reputation as an industry leader at a time when the developed world was obsessing over alternative energy sources and the exponentially increasing problem of plastic waste disposal. By devising a process which converts waste plastic into a premium grade combustible fuel, he cleverly positioned his firm on the international stage as a contributor to the alleviation of both these problems. Then he sold it, for a great deal of money.

James lives with his wife Ann and their much-loved dogs, Freddie a large, brown standard poodle and Kermit, their iron-grey French bulldog. Their two grown children are married and live nearby. James hates the word "retire" as it implies he has finished with life. In his mind, he was just warming up. Since leaping off the hamster wheel, he is now free to indulge in his passion for the outdoors.

For the past twenty years, James has spent as much of his spare time as possible participating in what he refers to as "adventuring", often alone. He does much of this adventuring in the Lake District and the Peak District, but whenever time and family commitments permit, James loves to travel further afield to the wild parts of Norway, Canada, the USA and Southern Europe. His favourite activities are mountain hiking, rock climbing, canoeing, competitive field archery and SCUBA diving.

James set up a WhatsApp group, inviting his three friends Drew Jackson, Simon Lee and Nick Thomson to join what he labelled The Wednesday Club. His objective was to ensure that they did something adventurous, or at the very least interesting, at least once a week. His three Wednesday Club comembers were also in the fortunate position of having significant free time. All four would object to the use the word "fortunate", they all shared the same cliched response to any suggestion of luck; "the harder I worked the luckier I became".

As for the three other members of the Wednesday Club:

Drew Jackson had been a fireman for twenty-five years. He retired from the service at the age of forty-seven and now runs a small but lucrative IT consulting business, having diligently studied and qualified for his new career in his spare time. He is careful not to overload himself with work as he insists on leaving enough time for his recreational interests, particularly hill walking, rock climbing and canoeing. His typical schedule entails working two long days per week, freeing up five days a week for himself.

Drew is single again. After twenty-two years of marriage, his now ex-wife took her substantial slice of his hard-earned retirement pie, eight months after he retired from the fire service. She demanded a divorce on the grounds of "having grown apart" but you can read into that, "I've found someone else". Their only child, Scott, is away studying at Cardiff University, leaving Drew to dodge the spectre of loneliness. He jumped enthusiastically into the activities of the Wednesday Club.

Drew is passionate about wildlife. He volunteers as a warden for the Northern Wildlife and Wilderness Conservation Trust, whose mission is to provide protected habitats, where wildlife can flourish unmolested by humans.

Simon Lee is forty-six years old. He lives with his wife Deb and his two teenage sons. He owns a scientific instrument business, which refurbishes and sells equipment to industry and academia. Simon leads major sales initiatives and manages financial matters. His small team of employees takes care of day to day business, leaving Simon with an abundance of leisure time. The Wednesday Club provides a welcome source of excitement in antidote to his work-weariness.

Simon is the steady-Eddie of the group. He applies thought and logic to everything he does. An approach that serves as a useful, moderating influence on the often impulsive and sometimes reckless behaviour of James and Drew.

Simon's favourite pastime is long distance trail hiking, in the UK and internationally.

Nick Thomson, at thirty-nine years of age, is the youngest of the group. In his own words:

"Well, in a nutshell, I'm not even forty yet, but I've bought two houses for two women. I worked on contract as a professional project manager in the oil sector, based in Aberdeen. I earned a significant sum of money, which fed an extravagant lifestyle. After the ex-wives cleared off with all my Worldly goods, what's mine is there's and so on, the tax man swooped in and skimmed up what was left. Whenever I have accumulated any amount of money, or come to that, property, there is always someone waiting to take it from me. So, my life style is now based on the premise that if I have nothing, no one can take it away from me."

Nick now lives alone above a pub on the outskirts of Manchester and has no plans to change that. His girlfriend of sixteen months walked out without a backward glance two months ago, following what Nick now jokingly refers to as a slight misunderstanding.

He has turned his back on the stresses of running engineering projects for big oil companies and now earns a living as a barman, working just downstairs from his small suite of rooms above the Colliers Arms. He spends everything he earns on entertaining himself. Memories and experience can neither be taxed nor spirited away by ruthless women.

His most prized possession is his Airdrop mountain bike, which he rides in off-road trail competitions. He has never won a race, but prides himself in always finishing in the first twenty percent of riders. His best position was third, in a field of thirty-seven.

The Wednesday Club's real value to its four like-minded members, is to bring an element of excitement, usually with a tinge of danger, as an antidote to the tame, overregulated society in which they live. Their attitude is nicely summed up by James's opinion on roller coaster rides; "They're ok, but not exactly exciting, as the outcome is always entirely predictable. No matter how many stomach-churning loops and drops you get, you know for sure that you'll be stepping safely out of the carriage in a matter of minutes. There's no risk involved and it takes no effort or thought on your part."

CHAPTER 3

The Seed is Sown

It's the 6th of June 2018.

James collected Simon, Drew and Nick at their respective homes around Manchester. The boot space of his Land Rover Discovery was soon crammed with hiking gear and a change of clothes for their customary, post walk pub visit.

They planned to spend the night in the Priest's Hole cave on Dove Crag in the Lake District and to make an early start from there, to walk the popular hiking route known as the Fairfield Horseshoe. This circular mountain hike traverses a variety of mountain terrain including grassy ridges, stony plateaus and rocky crag tops. Fairfield's plateau connects two major ridges North of Ambleside, taking in eight peaks and giving spectacular views of Rydal Water, Grasmere, Windermere and Ullswater.

The Priest's Hole was an unusual starting point for the walk, the more usual option being the nearby town of Ambleside.

James, Simon and Drew were all seasoned hill walkers, having hiked most of the UK's major hills and mountains over the past fifteen years or so. Nick was a newcomer to the activity, although he was confident that his fitness and stamina was up to the task as he was a regular long-distance cyclist. As the youngest member of the group, at a youthful age of thirty-nine Nick was jokingly referred to by the others as "the kid".

At 3.30 p.m. James parked his Land Rover at the public car park at Cow Bridge, near the tiny Cumbrian village of Hartsop.

James: "Right; we've got 2 hours to get our arses up to the Priest's Hole before complete darkness".

Their walk initially skirted the West side of Brothers Water to its Southern tip, from where they followed the course of Dovedale Beck, a lively mountain stream which feeds into the small lake. The low-level part of the route passes through typical Cumbrian valley farmland until a gradual incline marks the beginning of the ascent proper, starting with a steady slog up alternating boggy and rocky terrain. They skirted a series of waterfalls which cascade through craggy gullies flanked with ferns and stunted holly, rowan and juniper trees. The final climb to the point where Dovedale blends into the imposing rock face of Dove Crag is a steep gully scramble over loose rocks and scree. They found that the best way to ascend this section was to cling to the steep rock sides of the gully, avoiding the awkward alternative of slipping one step backwards for every two steps forward progress.

Nick: "Are you lot trying to kill me? you said we'd be walking up a path."

James, laughing: "This IS a path, it's marked on the map. What were you expecting tarmac and concrete steps?"

Nick: "I'm not sure really but I've not seen anything that even vaguely resembles a path since we left the car, we've scrambled up waterfalls and loose rock so far. And while I'm on one; why is it called hill-walking? This is mountaineering in my book. This cave had better be a four-star job with showers and feather pillows."

From a distance, the Priest's Hole, located two thirds up the sheer face of Dove Crag, looked impossibly inaccessible. Once they reached the top of the gully, narrow, stony paths and grassy ledges giving access to the cave came into view. They arrived at the cave entrance just as darkness swept across the mountains.

The light from headtorches rummaged from the depths of their rucksacks illuminated the dank interior of the cave. They surveyed the cramped space for suitable pitches for their mats and sleeping bags.

James produced a large, gift-boxed bottle of Bishop's Finger beer from his rucksack.

Simon: "That's a heavy drink to lug all the way up here mate. I've brought a bottle of Glenfiddich, almost ten times the bang for yer buck, well for the pack weight at least".

James: "Yes but think about where we are. This beer's appropriate to our location."

Drew, splurting out a mouthful of coffee: "Bloody hell James, your sense of humour hasn't changed much since we were at school, has it?"

Simon produced four small plastic cups from his rucksack and shared out the Glenfiddich whisky.

Nick: "So What do we do now?"

Drew: "When we've finished this whisky we'll pop out for a kebab."

Nick: "Really? Great, I'm starving. Where from?"

Drew: "I'm joking mate. We're stuck in here 'till morning, so you'd better eat your butties. You have brought food for tonight and tomorrow haven't you?"

Nick: "Ah. Yeah course I have."

James, his in-built mother hen pecking away at the inside of his skull: "It's worth remembering that we're on the side of a crag, so when you go out for a pee, don't forget how narrow the path is. If you do fall off, don't forget to shout before you hit the bottom."

The conversation followed the usual course; recounting past trips, stag parties, football and women. It then strayed off onto a new tangent.

Simon: "Do you know what really pisses me off?"

James: "What?"

Simon: "Injustice. Us decent, reasonably law-abiding people always get the shitty end of the stick, while the real bastards seem to get away with anything."

Nick: "Like what mate?"

Simon: "I'll give you a personal example; about nine months ago, some idiot bumped into Deb's car at the top of Church Street. He admitted that he was at fault and they swapped details. For six months our insurers tried to contact him and couldn't get any response, then he finally replied through a claims company and lo and behold he had conjured up a witness. A scrote who was prepared to stand up in Court to say he saw Deb roll back into his car. Our insurers backed us the whole way, Deb went to Court and because she had no witness and this prick had produced one, the idiot judge just gave the decision to him. He even won his claim for whiplash compensation. It was such an obvious a stitch-up that the insurance company didn't even hit Deb's no claims discount."

Drew: "Bastard."

Simon: "Deb was gutted, she had been made to look like a liar in Court. I collared the prick in the Court toilets and put the shits up the bastard. I told him I was going to sort his life out for calling my wife a liar. But in reality I can't do a thing, because I'll end up in deep shit. In fact, I was lucky to get away with just venting off at him like that, intimidation is a big no-no in Court."

James: "Wouldn't it be great to be able to call in a good Karma kicking on bastards like him? It's a great feeling to take revenge for something that has really pissed you off. A few years ago, I did a funny revenge job on someone. For about eight weeks we'd been finding huge piles of dog shit on our drive in the morning. I was really pissed off and was determined to catch the dirty bastard responsible; the owner not the dog. I decided to sit up one night and keep watch. I sat looking out of the front window with a couple of bottles of beer for company. I dozed off at about two a.m. and woke again at around six, I was just about to call it a night and go to bed when I saw a guy with a fat Labrador mooching around and sure enough it proceeded to dump its payload on my drive. I jumped up, threw my trainers and jacket on and sneaked out when the guy and his dog moved on. I followed them at a distance for about half a mile until they got home. I made a mental note of the address and plotted my revenge."

Simon: "What did you do?"

James: Laughing. "It was excellent. I collected three days' worth of Freddie's crap from my garden. And Freddie's a big dog so there was quite a hefty load of the stuff, a good couple of kilos. I waited until about two am on a Sunday morning and deposited Freddie's turds on the guy's windscreen and, even better, I plastered some up into his car door handle. I made the punishment fit the crime. An eye for an eye. I would love to have been a fly on the wall when he saw his car and then when he opened the door. It was so satisfying to look him in the eye when I saw him a few days later. I said "good morning" to him when I walked past with Freddie and I think he put two and two together. I turned around after we passed and saw him looking back at me in an odd way. The good thing is that he obviously suspects it was my doing as we no longer get his dog shit on our drive, but he will never be one hundred percent sure."

James rooted a couple of candles out of his rucksack, propped them on a rock ledge in the dark recess at the back of the cave and lit them. The glow they produced provided just enough light for the guys to set up their sleeping bags and mats and to brew tea on James's lightweight gas stove.

The four slept fitfully, frequently turning in their sleeping bags to try to get relief from the pressure points, where the rock floor of the cave pushed its gnarly knuckles through the thin padding of their bedding.

The entrance to the Priest's Hole faces East, its elongated, elliptical entrance gives the impression of a weary eye overseeing Dovedale and Brothers Water. As morning broke, the rising sun lit the cave's interior and prompted the group into crawling out of their sleeping bags like reluctant moths emerging from their cocoons. A temperature inversion had filled the valleys with a sea of cloud. Hartsop and St Sunday Crag ridges pierced through the cloud layer, to bask in the morning sun. The prospect of the day ahead motivated them into quickly dressing, eating their breakfasts of packaged instant meals and repacking their rucksacks ready for the off.

After a short scramble down from the cave to the approach gully and then upwards onto the rocky escarpment of Dove Crag, they joined the ridge-top path towards Hart Crag. At eight hundred and twenty-two metres this is the second highest point of the route.

The four guys made their way in an anti-clockwise direction around the Fairfield Horseshoe, enjoying the cold fresh air and eagerly absorbing the three-hundred-and-sixty-degree mountain panorama courtesy of a clear, bright morning.

The conversation wound back to the previous night's theme:

Drew: "I spent half the night trying to ignore all the snoring and farting. I lay awake mulling over what we were talking about last night, you know, karma and all that. Why should we take shit from morons and just let it go?"

Simon: "What do you mean? James didn't let it go."

Drew: "No, I'm not talking about the dog shit scenario. That was an excellent response by James, but really that was pretty lightweight stuff. I'm talking more about people crapping on you from a great height and just walking away with impunity. Like the idiot that pranged your Deb's car, not only did he get away with it, but he was actually financially rewarded for his lies and deceit."

Nick: "The key is plausible deniability and anonymity. We should arrange to deal with each other's issues, so the affected person can maintain a distance. Don't shit on your own doorstep and all that."

Simon: "Ha, yeah that would be great. The thought of you three dishing up revenge on mine and Deb's behalf is quite appealing. Like Karma Police…. wasn't that a song by Radiohead?"

James: "Well let's do it. We have the time and, apparently, the inclination. We're always looking for the next idea for a stimulating challenge".

And so, the seed was sown.

Over the next five kilometres of ridge walk they contemplated the modus operandi of the group. They jointly and jokingly came up with less than ten commandments, which of course, according to commandment number one, would never be written down or recorded.

Wednesday Club Karma Commandments:
- Nothing is to be recorded in any way, hard copy or digital. All details must be committed to memory
- There must be one hundred percent certainty about the offence and the identity of the perpetrator
- An eye for an eye. The nature of the retribution is to be proportionate with the offence and must reflect or represent in some way the type of crime committed by the perpetrator

- Without risking exposing our identities, whenever possible the targeted perpetrators should be able to figure out the reason they had been served up retribution
- The Wednesday Club member(s) serving up justice must have no direct or indirect connections to the perpetrator
- Whenever possible the retribution must be amusing. We need to get a laugh out of this. And the act must be seen by the whole group
- If any member is questioned about any activity: deny, deny, deny and never pass on any information about other members

As they continued their walk, Simon had been mulling over their new plan to expand the scope of their Wednesday Club activities: "Sounds like fun, but do you not think we'd be overstepping the line into crazy territory?"

James: "Yes, absolutely. That's the attraction of it, the World needs crazy. Where would humankind be without craziness? I'm not claiming that we'll be making a major contribution to society, but we humans would still be sat on our arses in caves and stick huts if history wasn't peppered with insane stunts undertaken by the mad and the brave. Imagine Captain Cook setting off on his explorations, not having a clue where he would end up or whether he and his crew were sailing to their deaths. I'm sure most people would have thought he was a proper nutjob, but he discovered Hawaii and was the first European to land on Australia's East coast.

Simon, laughing: "Yes, but didn't he end up as the main course on some Polynesian island?"

James: "Not quite. He was clubbed to death on a beach in Hawaii."

Nick: "And how different things might have been, if Sir Francis Drake hadn't decided to set fire to half his fleet and sail right into the Spanish Armada."

Simon: "Yes, point taken. Let's do it."

With that discussion, the four Wednesday Club members agreed that the idea was "a goer" and that Karma distribution would feature among their activities.

CHAPTER 4

Riverside Plot

It is now the 18th of October 2018.

James, Drew, Nick and Simon were stood around a brick-built barbeque outside a tipi in a field in Herefordshire. Having washed down smoke blackened burgers and sausages with numerous bottles of beer from the cool box, they stoked and poked the charcoal, to push back the chill of the night. The sky was clear and awash with stars. This was the end of day one of a three-day camping and canoeing trip on the most scenic stretches of the River Wye.

James: "OK, we've mulled over the idea of the Wednesday Club karma delivery service for months now. If we're going to do this, let's each of us make a suggestion for a mission. I suggest we take Simon's car crash case up as the first, as that clearly demands some retribution. Agreed?"

All agreed that as Simon had been the first to provide details of a deserving case then he should be the first to benefit from the door to door karma service.

They decided to retreat into the tipi in the hope that its interior would be warmer than the outside. It wasn't. A cold chill wafted in through gaps around its base.

Drew: "Whose idea was it to do this trip in October? What's wrong with July?"

James: "October's supposed to be a good month for river water levels, after the dry months of summer."

Simon: "Well its bloody freezing."

Nick: "I guarantee that the river is colder, so let's hope we manage to keep our canoes upright tomorrow."

Simon: "Nick, you never did tell me why Sally walked out on you."

Nick: "Well its quite funny really. It wasn't at the time, but looking back at it…. Let's just say that having got home after a lovely night out in Didsbury, we'd cosied down on the couch, when I inadvertently called Sally "Ellie", the name of my previous girlfriend. There was an awkward silence for a few seconds then she got up, put on her shoes and stormed out in a right huff. We haven't spoken since. That girl has no sense of humour."

Simon: "Never mind mate. Plenty more fish in the sea and all that."

Nick: "Well plenty fish on Tinder anyway. It hadn't exactly been domestic bliss, so no big loss. I think she had an agenda that I wouldn't have been prepared to buy into."

One by one, the guys dropped off to sleep as the beer took effect.

In the morning they ate their usual lazy breakfast of packaged camping meals and tea heated over propane stoves.

After plastic breakfast dishes had been washed, dried and stored, Nick and Simon put on their buoyancy aids and loaded up their rented two-man Canadian canoe with dry-bags full of food, drinks and spare clothes. They then launched the canoe into the speedy flow of the River Wye. James and Drew followed in James's own seventeen-foot inflatable kayak, known affectionately as The Grey Whale.

They paddled along the scenic stretch of the river which passes Goodrich Castle. The scenery here is beautiful, idyllic British countryside. Later that morning, due to the looping course of the river, they twice passed by the impressive precipice of Symonds Yat Rock, first on its Eastern flank and then along its West side. In addition to the imposing scenery of this part of the Wye valley, the area is also famous for the discovery of fossils of hyenas, sabre toothed cats and mammoths in its many caves. Reminders of this country's ancient, wilder past.

Three hours of relaxed paddling was followed by lunch stop at an ancient, riverside inn at Symonds Yat. This was the perfect place for refuelling tired muscles and for a couple, or so, beers to provide additional confidence for their attempt on the famous, grade-two Symonds Yat rapids. By the third beer any apprehension about tackling the rapids in unwieldy canoes had been pissed down the drain and they eagerly returned to the muddy river bank, untied their boats and pushed off into the flow.

The water moved quickly through the rapids, thanks to a solid week of rain falling just prior to the trip. Nick and Simon went first, paddling tentatively until they were drawn by the turbulent, tea coloured current, which accelerated them relentlessly past the point of no return. "Don't forget; paddle like bastards" came the advice jokingly shouted by James, who was watching from his upstream vantage point in the grey whale. Ignoring his advice, on entering the rapids Nick and Simon lifted their paddles out of the water, believing that this would slow their progress and make for an easier passage through the turbulent flow. This was the worst thing they could have done. They lost directional control.

Their canoe was pushed sideways onto a car sized rock and bounced off to spin in a one-hundred-and-eighty-degree pirouette. Realising their mistake, Nick and Simon paddled hard in their attempt to point the canoe back in the right direction, resulting in clawing drag from the water flow gripping its left side, pulling it over and dunking the two occupants on the upstream side of the canoe. Their bodies reacted automatically to the unexpected immersion in the frigid water, they both gasped involuntarily, filling lungs to capacity with air. Fortunately, their reflex gasps came after their heads had reappeared above the surface, so they gulped in air rather than water.

Clinging on to the partly submerged boat until it entered slower water, they were able to swim to a safe eddy out of the main current, dragging their canoe with them. After a few seconds of thought gathering, teeth chattering with cold, Nick ran downstream along the river bank to drag ejected drybags and paddles from the river, while Simon tipped the canoe over to drain it.

Having watched Nick and Simon's drama, James and Drew entered the rapids enthusiastically and paddled at a fast pace. The current played around with the clumsy inflatable kayak and they too were soon travelling backwards along the choppy flow. After a few well-timed and coordinated switches of paddling effort from one side of the boat to the other, they managed to realign their bow into the direction of flow and bounced along to the end of the rapids. They offered smug, triumphant smiles to their drenched mates as they exited the main flow into the eddy to join them on the bank.

Nick and Simon hastily changed into dry clothes from the rescued drybags and soon both boats were relaunched to continue the journey.

Symonds Yat rapids is quite a short stretch of water, but it is followed by around a mile of choppy water, which proved to be just as much fun as the "main event". By late afternoon, the group made it without further drama to Monmouth, where they hauled the canoes out, dragging them up the boating club's concrete steps. From here, men and boats were transported by their trip organisers back to the tipi site for their last night of the voyage.

At the tipi site, in a repeat of the previous night's procedure, out came the cool box and the barbeque was lit once more. The beer was now warmer than it had been on the previous night, but no less welcome.

James: "Ok, we need to arrange the details and timing of our first karma mission on behalf of Simon and, without her knowledge of course, for Deb' too."

Over the next three hours, before a sudden and unexpected rain shower sent them off once again to the relative warmth of their sleeping bags, the four fledgling agents of Karma plotted their first mission.

CHAPTER 5

Urban Trebuchet

4am. The 19th November 2018.

The day had come. The four Wednesday Club members were excited and apprehensive, in fact they were downright twitchy. No matter how much their target deserved this, their plan was in every way illegal and they all risked serious consequences if they were caught in the act or apprehended after the event.

Simon had provided all necessary details. The perpetrator was a window cleaner, Tommy Wilkinson, who lives in a small semidetached house on Bridgewater Street in Leyton, a small, tired looking suburb of Manchester.

Wilkinson's offence involved damage to Deb's car as well as her confidence, so retribution would focus on his car, a white Peugeot Estate, complete with roof rack and ladders. It was parked outside his house, its rear positioned very close to the front of his neighbour's car, so that the overhanging ladders presented an awkward obstacle to anybody wishing to walk between the two cars.

James, Nick and Drew had recced the house and surroundings three times over the past two weeks, twice on bikes, as cyclists usually attract little attention. They had established that Wilkinson's car should be parked at the front of his house until he left to start work between 7.30 a.m. and 8.00 a.m.

On the night of the operation, they returned to Bridgewater Street at 4.30 a.m. They had travelled here in Nick's car as it was the smallest of their vehicles, it was also dark in colour and so, hopefully wouldn't be very noticeable. They parked fifty metres or so from Wilkinson's house, surveyed the street for ten minutes to ensure there were no late-night dog walkers or curtain twitchers and then quietly exited the car to make their way to the target vehicle. All three wore high-viz vests. Sometimes the best way to avoid attention was to be conspicuous. Hiding in plain sight.

The front of the Peugeot was a few metres from the nearest vehicle, so the three group members could be confident that Wilkinson would walk around the front of his car to the driver's door, rather than having to limbo dance under his own ladders.

They had brought along a length of strong steel chain with hefty links and two heavy duty padlocks. Their initial idea had been to secure part of the car to a nearby lamppost, however on reassessing the job on the hoof, Drew noticed that the car was parked over an iron grid cover, so instead of looping the chain around the lamppost, they attached one end to the overhanging ladders with a padlock and fed the other end of the chain through the bars of the grid. After a minute or two's fiddling, using a twig from an overhanging tree, Nick managed to hook the dangling end of the chain back up through the grid. He then attached the second padlock securing the chain around one of the grid cover's bars. The idea would create an interesting tug-of-war contest. Car versus cast iron grid.

Nick ensured that the chain was in the most concealed location possible, tucking it in tightly along the shadow of the kerb and then passing it up to the ladders on the offside edge of the rear hatch of the vehicle. A couple of pieces of duct tape made sure the chain was held in place against the car.

The whole mission had taken only six and a half minutes. The three dubious avenging angels were once more seated in Nick's car. They drove away as quietly as possible to grab an early breakfast at the nearest all-night café.

Just after 7.00am they collected Simon from his house and the four of them then returned to Bridgewater Street, parking a few doors away from Wilkinson's house to eagerly and nervously witness the result of their night's mischief.

At 7.44am Wilkinson closed his front door behind him, ready to start his week's work cleaning the grime and pigeon shit off his customers' windows. He hated Monday's, "well doesn't everyone" he thought to himself.

He squeezed himself and his mug of coffee into the front seat of the Peugeot, placed the mug into the central cup holder and started up the engine. He sat revving his engine for a while, for no particular purpose other than to annoy his elderly neighbours. He resented "the old bastards" as he referred to them, enjoying a lie in, while he was having to sweat his way up and down ladders, soaked to the skin in cold, soapy water.

Wilkinson put the car into first gear and drove slowly away from the kerb without bothering to indicate his intentions to other road users that might have been nearby. His eyes widened and his jaw dropped into a fly-catching gape when he felt the rear of his car plunge downwards and simultaneously heard a shocking metallic clang as the ladders crushed his puny roof rack, collapsing it into the car roof. The next instant, the rear of the car Kangarooed, bouncing up on its rear suspension as the heavy grid cover catapulted upwards from its location, its seal of grime having been violently broken. The grid cover propelled upwards as if shot from a medieval trebuchet, slammed down on the car roof alongside the ladders and crunched a deep dent the size of a shoe box into the roof panel.

Wide-eyed, Wilkinson emerged slowly from the car as if just wakening from a nightmare. He stepped back from his car, staring at the damaged roof, while repeating over and over like a YouTube cockatoo "what the fuck, what the fuck.....". Ashen faced, he stood scratching his head, trying to absorb and rationalise what had just taken place.

James, Nick, Simon and Drew were transfixed for a few moments by the violent success of their mission. Then they quickly left the scene, driving past their confused, jabbering victim as the occupants of two nearby houses came out to investigate the source of the commotion. Simon couldn't help trying to catch Wilkinson's eyes as they drove past. He really wanted the satisfaction of the last twist of the knife. He wanted Wilkinson to know he was behind this.

They returned to James's house for a celebratory coffee and to reflect on the morning's misdeeds.

Drew: "Do you realise how risky that was? We could have killed him if he'd had a sunroof."

James: "Well luckily he didn't have a sunroof. All's well that ends well."

Simon: "I think we should be careful to think through potential consequences on any future karma missions."

James, laughing: "Yes, but we're not going to prepare risk assessments and call in the HSE for guidance. I tell you what we do need in future; concrete alibis established in advance and built into a rock- solid story. I saw you Simon, hoping Wilkinson would see you as we drove away."

Simon: "OK; our alibi for tonight is that we were all at yours James, playing cards through the night. We're all insomniacs; right?"

The Wednesday Club members spent the next ninety minutes fine tuning their alibis while playing poker in a light-hearted mood.

Simon: "Well thanks for the night's effort guys. I certainly feel justice has been served up on that arsehole. Perhaps he'll think twice in the future before crapping on people. The whole thing will probably be blamed on local kids pranking him. There are quite a few rum little shits around there."

James: "It was fun and it had a sense of purpose and justice. Anyway, who's next? Who has a good cause for our next mission?"

CHAPTER 6

Upping the Ante

Drew: "Well I've been mulling over my nomination for the last few days. It'll take some careful planning and we'd have to get up close and personal with a nasty piece of work, but I think this bastard is overdue some serious karma."

Drew went on to outline the offences of his proposed selection for target number two and the reasons for his nomination:

In his work for the Northern Wildlife and Wilderness Trust, Drew and some of his volunteer colleagues had had run-ins with his nominee, a gamekeeper for a pheasant shoot, based on an estate of over a hundred acres of woodland, open fields and moorland in Blackdog Clough in the Dark Peak area of the Peak District National Park.

Most game shoots in the Dark Peak are of the grouse variety, but the predominantly wooded habitat of this particular estate was more suited to pheasants. The shoot is adjacent to open moorland and adjoins the nature reserve that Drew patrolled once a week as a volunteer warden.

The Dark Peak is a spectacular wilderness situated close to England's centre, comprising remote mountain plateaus, gritstone crags, peat bogs and moorland. The area is historically fascinating and is also famous for its unique wildlife. It is home to England's only population of mountain hare, a smaller cousin of the more common brown hare, believed to have been stranded here by the retreat of the last ice-age. As winter approaches the hare morphs from brown to white, its small heat-conserving ears and large snow-shoe feet enable it to survive high up on the moors and mountains during the severe winter conditions of the Peak District.

Myths and legends of ghosts, strange creatures and even UFOs abound in the Dark Peak. Moonscape rock formations and haunting cries of moorland birds like the curlew contribute to the fantastic eeriness and timelessness of the place.

Wrecks of World War II aircraft still lie scattered across the Dark Peak, all of which have been picked to their metal skeletons by "collectors" illegally scavenging souvenirs.

Over the past four years, since Drew commenced his role for the NWWT, he had encountered the gamekeeper around a dozen times lurking within the reserve, which the Trust owned and maintained for the benefit of wildlife. Each time, Drew had explained forcefully to him that he was on a private reserve, which was a designated a SSSI (Site of Special Scientific Interest) and was excluded from the CRoW (Countryside and Rights of Way) act. As such he had been invited by Drew to "fuck off sharpish".

During the time he had been working at the reserve, Drew had made a few friends and contacts in the area. He frequented the two pubs in Hindhurst, the nearest village and had become well known as a regular face in the Greenman Hotel and the Lamb Inn. Drew had developed a good rapport with a few regulars and over time he had come to learn about the gamekeeper's character and habits. He had learned that he was a cruel and heartless man who wouldn't think twice about digging up young fox cubs from their den and throwing them to his dogs, just to "keep them keen". He arrogantly rebutted any criticism of his cruel habits as the complaints of townies who don't understand country ways.

The gamekeeper usually paraded around the village dressed in tweed jacket and cap, along with the obligatory green hunter wellies and spaniel at heel. His vain and deluded endeavour to be perceived as a respectable country gentleman, whatever that might be, failed to impress. Most of the locals considered him to be an ignorant imbecile. In his absence, he was often referred to by the regulars in the Greenman and the Lamb Inn as "The Rat", due to his rodent like appearance. His real name is Nigel Buxton. He happily answers to the nickname of "Buckie". Whether "Buckie" is derived from his surname or is in reference to his teeth, nobody is quite sure.

Drew: "He could pick olives out of a jar with his yellow, bucked teeth. And his feeble attempt at a moustache looks just like a rat's wiry whiskers. Bastard gives me the creeps."

Buckie was divorced and lived alone on the outskirts of Hindhurst. He rarely saw his daughter, who attended primary school in Sheffield and lived with her mother and step-father in Bamford.

While the pheasant shoot is on private land, the public has right of access thanks to the CRoW (Countryside and Rights of Way) act, although the shoot owners are allowed to exclude the public on shooting days. Drew had exploited his right to roam, in order to keep an eye open for any illegal or cruel activities being carried out on behalf of the shoot. During his forays he had observed from a distance, through his binoculars, Buckie setting illegal pole traps.

Pole traps are cruel devices consisting of a pair of hinged, toothed, metal jaws, operated by strong springs, designed to slam shut when a bird alights on it. The traps are baited and fixed to the tops of fence posts. They are undiscriminating and inhumane, their victims are left dangling by broken legs to die in agony.

Drew actively searched out these illegal killing devices, he often found them triggered, with their macabre trophies hanging limply from their jaws. He always removes the traps whenever he discovers them, but they are soon replaced. He has seen buzzards, short eared owls, goshawks and merlin caught in this way, all protected raptor species. Due to their natural inquisitiveness, crows are the most frequent victims of the traps.

Drew explained how this mindless killing got under his skin, he abhorred cruelty and the annihilation of these innocent creatures in the name of protecting the shoot's pheasant stock. If left in peace, these birds of prey would be responsible for very few game bird losses, their natural choice of prey being the indigenous small birds and mammals that inhabit the area.

The shoot breeds around two thousand pheasant each year. On shoot days they are scared into flight by beaters and spaniels to provide the hooray Henry "hunters" with the thrill of heroically blasting them from the sky with lead shot.

The estate's method of pheasant breeding is an unnatural process, entailing artificial incubation of bought-in eggs in heated cabins. Once hatched, the pheasants are crammed into pens for intensive feeding and dosing with antibiotics. By the time they mature, the birds are so tame and accepting of human presence that they need to be shooed away from their pens into the woods. There they are fed from grain hoppers until it is time for them to be slaughtered and maimed in the name of sport.

Drew felt enraged that no matter how well protected the birds of prey and other wildlife were while within the boundaries of the trust's reserve, once they flew, hopped or ran onto neighbouring land, they were immediately in peril. While the Trust could be proud of the successful nesting of rare raptors under their care and management, they felt helpless in preventing the birds being illegally shot or trapped once they left the safe confines of the reserve.

The Trust liaised with the police who provided some support by following up any suspected offences witnessed by trust members. However, the illegal activities of Buckie and his cohorts were usually carried out clandestinely, under cover of darkness when they could be confident that their actions would go unseen. Or so they thought.

Drew concluded his case by saying that game bird shooting is not the noble sport, keenly portrayed by its participants as man pitting his hunting skills against the wilderness to provide meat for the table. Most birds killed on the shoot don't end up on the dinner table. He had seen heaped carcasses of grouse and pheasant left to rot in ditches.

Nick: "Wow Drew, I didn't know you were so into wildlife conservation and all that stuff. It sounds like this gamekeeper is a right evil shit."

Drew: "Yes, it sickens me to the stomach that the sick pastime of a few rich idiots, is allowed to cause such devastation to wildlife. A recently published scientific paper links the massive decline in hen harrier numbers with moorland grouse shoots. Hen harriers are amazing birds, you should see their aerobatic sky-dancing displays over the moors. Another tragic example; gamekeepers were responsible for driving the Scottish wildcat near to extinction. Of course, the sick shooting fraternity still try to deny any connection."

Drew looked at the attentive faces of his friends and a smile erased the sternness that had occupied his face as he spoke with such passion. "Sorry if that was a bit of a soapbox speech, but I get so wound   up   by   this   shit."

Nick: "So I see. What's the plan then Drew, what do we need to achieve."

Drew: "Well what I would really like to do is to scare the bastard half to death, make him fear for his life and convince him that if he continues needlessly destroying wildlife, he will face some serious consequences."

Nick, grinning: "We could tar and feather him, pheasant feathers of course. Give him a minute's start on the moors and hunt him down. Poetic justice, Lord of The Flies style."

Simon: "You're really fuming at this guy aren't you Drew?"

Drew: "Yep. He must be stopped. Trouble is there are a thousand more arseholes like him up and down the country."

James: "OK that gives us all plenty of scope to use our imagination. I already have some ideas whizzing around my head. Let's fine tune a plan over a few beers on our next Wednesday Club trip."

CHAPTER 7

A Plot Hatches

16th January 2019. The Wednesday Club members are back in the Lake District

The picturesque seventeenth century Packhorse Inn in the Cumbrian parish of Mungrisdale was the perfect location from which to start their planned route in the morning. A route that would take them over the famous Sharp Edge, onto the summit of Blencathra, in an exciting scramble with exposed drop offs.

In the morning, the four mates eagerly ploughed through their full English breakfast. Cumberland sausage, eggs and bacon helped to soak up the one too many pints of draught real ale they had downed the previous night, while plotting their next mission. The rest would be sweated out on the walk.

Drew's gamekeeper nominee had now been formally accepted as their next target.

Over their beers, the four had quietly hatched a plot designed to deliver the requisite mix of retribution and persuasion that Drew hoped for. The mission will entail face to face confrontation. A new, exciting and perturbing concept for the group.

Satisfied with the meticulous, military style planning of their next mission, they now set off to enjoy their latest adventure.

Below a threatening, thunder grey sky, a wind swept in from the North, whipping snow across the hills. Even at valley level the terrain was white over. They set off, trudging through soft snow, following the winding course of the River Glendermackin, heading against the direction of its flow towards Scales Tarn. As they gained height the surface of the snow developed a crust of ice which thickened with altitude. By the time they reached the tarn their boots were no longer breaking through the freezing snow crust and they were able to make easy progress by kicking into the sparkling white surface of the snow. They paused briefly for a pit-stop at Scales Tarn, refuelling on jelly babies, crisps and frigid water. Here they also "kitted up" for the climb, attaching crampons to boots, securing ice axe leashes to wrists and cinching up rucksack straps. Sharp Edge in full Winter condition was a serious undertaking, requiring a good head for heights and careful manoeuvring across ice covered rock.

North of Scales Tarn the track makes its way along the top of a narrowing ridge, from where the knife-edged arete of Sharp Edge rises imposingly between two valleys that had been scooped from ancient rock by glaciers during the last ice age.

This was the perfect day to experience the spectacular and daunting exposure of the route. Looking ahead, the gleaming white crest of the ridge disappeared into the slate grey cloud ceiling. It was easy to imagine it stretching ever upwards to the outer reaches of the atmosphere.

The four guys made their way along the airy ridge, taking care with each step to ensure the points of their crampons were biting firmly into the ice, to avoid taking a deadly tumble.

This was Nick's first foray into the mountains in such challenging conditions. His three companions detected from his nervous mutterings and the heightened pitch of his voice that he was becoming edgy about their exposed situation. Words of encouragement and advice were offered:

Drew: "Don't forget to maintain three points of contact."

Simon: "Awesome up here isn't it. Not often you see the edge in such excellent condition."

They would soon reach the notorious "Bad Step," the crux move of the route which entails manoeuvring around a tilted, cow-sized rock pinnacle by stepping precariously onto a narrow, sloping ledge. The ledge has been polished shiny by thousands of boots and it tilts disconcertingly towards an immense drop into a rocky abyss. The Bad Step is followed by a steep drop down into a notch in the ridge, before the line of Sharp Edge ascends once again.

The Bad Step has claimed many lives. The local mountain rescue team refer to the adjacent chasm as "the usual gully" because most victims of Sharp Edge are discovered there.

They were now in the cloud. Visibility was equivalent to that of a 1950's London pea soup fog. Sounds became muffled. Their voices echoed eerily off the crag faces.

The muted voices of another party could be heard heading towards them, they were using Sharp Edge as their descent route from Blencathra. The climbers appeared ghost-like out of the mist fifteen metres ahead, then a millisecond later they were struck by disaster. One member of the oncoming party slipped and fell headlong down the northern flank of the ridge. Fortunately; a rock pinnacle broke his fall five metres below. Unfortunately; that same pinnacle snapped his femur with a sickening crack, which was immediately followed by a haunting, animal scream from the victim.

The Wednesday Club members froze for an instant. James shouted to the other group that they were on their way to help. By the time they reached the scene of the incident, some of the victim's friends had already lowered themselves to the victim and were providing first aid. There were six members in the victim's party and a brief conversation convinced James, Nick, Simon and Drew that the other group was confident and competent in dealing with the disaster without additional assistance. Three would stay with the victim to provide reassurance, first aid, warmth and food. The other two were tasked with calling out mountain rescue and guiding them to their location.

There was no signal from any of their phones, so they planned to retrace their steps back to the top of the mountain in the hope that they would pick up a signal there. Failing that, they would head back down as fast as conditions would allow, to summon help once a signal appeared. They knew that the nearby village of Scales was served by a phone signal as they had used their phones while visiting the White Horse Inn there.

On witnessing the shocking incident, the Wednesday Club members felt chilled to the bones. Not because of the cold mountain air that surrounded them, they were accustomed to that, this was the raw chill of fear, brought on by hearing a grown man scream like a child as the mountain claimed him as its latest victim. They stood motionless, quietly composing themselves. The haunting, hollow "cronk, cronk" cries of ravens echoed around them from the crags, the calls of these huge, black birds of the mountains muted into eerie sound shadows by the heavy mist.

They still had to negotiate the Bad Step, which now seemed a much more daunting prospect than it had done a few minutes earlier.

Drew: "OK, are we all ready to move on?"

Simon: "Yes, let's just take our time and tread very carefully."

Nick froze to the spot: "I'm not going across that tricky bit, I'd rather turn back."

James: "It's more dangerous going down Sharp Edge than up it."

Nick: "Yes, but after seeing that poor sod tumble off, I just don't want to risk the Bad Step."

They deliberated for a while, James, Simon and Drew calming and reassuring Nick. They agreed that James would set up a fixed rope belay on the steep section of crag above the notch. That way he could protect the others as they made their way across this tricky section.

While James was attaching Nick to the rope and setting up the belay, Simon and Drew, declining the added security offered by a rope, cautiously and nimbly crossed the Bad Step and made their way to a ledge a couple of metres above James's position. There they jammed their ice axes into cracks in the rock to provide extra security, while they waited for Nick to cross.

James shouted to Nick to "climb when ready". Being attached to a rope, which was secured both to James and to the mountain, gave Nick the confidence to move across the most precarious section of the ridge without further hesitation. When Nick arrived at James's side, James untied him and coiled the rope. Nick was now perched on a ledge which was a comfortable width, there was almost enough space for both his feet.

James noticed Nick's left leg was shaking and decided to make light of it. "I see you've got a touch of Elvis leg mate."

Nick replied "Elvis leg; what the hell's that?"

James just smiled and pointed towards Nick's trembling knee. "Ah, that." replied Nick sheepishly.

After the rope was consigned back into the depths of James's rucksack, they made short work of the remainder of Sharp Edge. A steep scramble up the face of Foule Crag took them to the top of the ridge where the mountain plateaued into a more benign mound. While their minds had been fully occupied by the task of safely completing the ridge climb, they hadn't noticed that the wind had whipped up and was now blowing at around fifty mph, bringing heavy snow with it.

As a result of the deteriorating weather the group had to walk at a crouch, leaning into the wind while trying to shield their faces from the sting of the high velocity, horizontal snow. This was a proper whiteout.

Their original plan had been to descend Blencathra via Hall's Fell Ridge, which is almost as exposed and challenging as Sharp Edge. The guys quickly agreed a plan B, taking a more straightforward and less exposed way down via Scales Fell.

Due to the whiteout, which reduced visibility to around five metres, navigating was seriously challenging and slowed progress significantly. In high winds it is all too easy to inadvertently stray off a compass bearing, particularly on sloping terrain. The four guys used a leap-frogging navigation technique, using back-bearing compass readings to ensure accuracy of direction. Employing this method significantly slows progress but improves precision.

The four were so focused on safely navigating their way off the mountain that the only words spoken for the next half hour were those needed to coordinate the effort.

Once they were on easier ground, having pinpointed the narrow ridgeline which exits Blencathra's summit eastwards between precipitous crags, they relaxed and conversation wandered back to the traumatic incident they had witnessed on the ascent. That drama would still be unfolding. In weather like this, it would be impossible for a helicopter to be deployed, therefore the Mountain Rescue team would have to rush to the scene on foot. They estimated that it would probably be at least four hours before the unfortunate guy with the broken leg was safely off the mountain.

Nick then hesitantly brought up another subject: "Sorry about losing it back there guys. I don't know what came over me."

Drew: "Yeah, you pussy!........... Just kidding mate, we were all spooked by that poor guy taking a dive, and don't forget, you haven't done this sort of Winter scrambling before."

Simon: "No shame in being cautious mate. Everybody has their limit and if you reach it, you shouldn't be shy in saying so."

James: "You're a competitive mountain biker. I've seen the speed you hurtle down hills without slowing down for bends. I'm sure the rest of us would be burning our brakes the whole way down. It's horses for courses mate. Don't worry; no one's going to question the size of your nuts."

CHAPTER 8

Crows Hatch

Late January 2019

The team worked on the basis that preparation is everything. Leading up to their latest mission, the Wednesday Club members had taken turns to covertly familiarise themselves with the activities of the gamekeeper, Buckie. A newly acquired, powerful infra-red night vision scope enabled them to watch undetected from a distance. Having built up a picture of Buckie's routine and activities, they carefully decided on the location and timing of their new karma delivery mission.

It transpired that Buckie was a creature of habit. Every Tuesday, Thursday and Sunday evening, at around 7.30 p.m. he would drive his scruffy, old, white transit van, to a cabin complex at the edge of the woods. There he would park up and eat a packed meal, read the paper, lock up his van, check around the cabins and then head off to patrol the land that comprised the shoot. The cabins were obviously some sort of office and HQ, central to the pheasant shoot's operations.

Buckie's first priority on his rounds was to visit the pole traps he had fixed along the fence which separates the shoot's woods from its moorland section. He would triumphantly remove his latest victims to suspend them from the barbed wire in a grotesque ritual. The fence was adorned with bird carcasses in varying stages of decay, like a witch's washing line.

On witnessing Buckie's cruelty on his lone recces, Drew found it very difficult to hold back from taking immediate offensive action. He reminded himself that patience and restraint were required if their plot was to succeed. He took some comfort in the fact that this discovery and planning stage of the operation was merely a prelude to meting out punishment and to what should be an effective disruption of the gamekeeper's repulsive activities.

After pegging out the pole trap victims, mostly crows but also the occasional rare raptor, Buckie would make his way down to the woods and disappear into the largest of the five cabins. This cabin housed his office and part-time living quarters, which he occupied during intense periods of activity in breeding and shooting seasons. According to their door labels, the other four cabins were used for pheasant incubation and rearing.

Electricity was provided to the cabins by large, run and standby, diesel powered generators, located in a roofed, open-sided shelter a few metres from the complex of cabins. In addition to providing heating and lighting to Buckie's temporary living quarters, the generators were essential to the successful raising of pheasants from egg to fledged chicks.

The group had given careful thought to concealing their activities and covering their tracks. Alibi's had been thoroughly rehearsed. The scope of this mission would certainly cross the line into serious unlawful territory.

Unlike Scotland, wild camping in England and Wales in is not a legal right. It is tolerated in some areas of the Lake District National Park, if carried out considerately in high and remote locations. The Peak District however is a different kettle of fish. Wild camping is not tolerated here, offenders can expect to be moved on as soon as they are spotted by rangers or landowners. However; James knew of a suitable spot, which was rarely visited because it lies within an area marked on Ordnance Survey maps as "The Swamp", giving the impression that it is inaccessible and dangerous ground. The price for the guarantee of privacy was a lengthy walk to the chosen location of their planned confrontation with Buckie in the remote valley of Blackdog Clough.

The four Wednesday Club members would spend three days wild camping in The Swamp. As far as family and friends were concerned, they would be out of phone signal range and so, as Drew put it "just like in the good old days" they would be isolated from the wider World. They were uncontactable and more importantly unlocatable, as phones would be switched off from the moment they left the car. This was part of their alibi construction. Four law-abiding guys on a camping trip. Guilty only of the minor, inadvertent transgression of camping without the landowner's permission.

They parked James's Land Rover in a car park in the Derbyshire market town of Glossop, which is known as the gateway to the Peak District. It was possible to park much closer to their destination, however a vehicle parked in a layby on Snake Pass for a few days would probably draw unwanted attention from National Trust Rangers or thieves.

At dusk they loaded themselves up like biped pack-mules with all the kit they needed for a three-day wild camp and for their karma mission. Even with their choice of ultralight camping gear they were still lugging fifteen kilos each. They carried a minimal amount of water, as they could use filter bottles to provide drinkable water from even the most turbid pools and streams. Drew likes to remind the others that if they were desperate, using the filter bottles they could even drink their own piss, filtered of course. He claimed to have tried it.

Faces spattered by windblown, sleety, wet snow, the four walked quietly through streets lined with sandstone buildings. The roads and footpaths glistened yellow with reflections from street lights. They passed by shops, cafés and pubs to the eastern outskirts of town. A fox paused his kebab recycling work as they passed, a front paw nervously raised in readiness until the threat had passed.

On entering the inky blackness of open moorland the temperature dropped noticeably. A patchwork covering of snow reflected the moonlight.

Navigating across featureless moorland requires focused concentration, so conversation was limited to the task in hand. To avoid drawing attention to themselves, head torches remained in rucksacks and they relied on their own night vision, assisted by watery light from an almost full moon. For most of the eight kilometres trudge to their chosen camp site, the moorland terrain squelched underfoot and with each step, black peaty mud squirted up the legs of the Wednesday Club members as they marched with grim determination, like four horseless apocolytes.

Drew: "Did you know that this part of the Dark Peak is supposed to be one of the most haunted places in Britain?"

Nick: "You don't believe in that crap do you?"

Drew: "You never know. There have been tons of reports from people claiming to have seen a Roman legion on Bleaklow, always in the same area. The soldiers are said to march across the moor carrying burning torches, from the site of Melandra, an old roman fort near Glossop…..And then there's Owd Schuck, the black ghost dog that's regularly seen wandering the lanes around Edale."

Simon: "Well thanks for that Drew; that's me not sleeping for the next three nights."

On reaching The Swamp, skirting the boggiest ground, they searched around for a suitable hollow in which they could conceal their tents from the view of any walkers crossing Bleaklow, on one of the remotest and most challenging sections of the Pennine Way.

They found a relatively dry patch of ground amongst the bogs and pools that earned The Swamp its name. Here they pitched their four tiny backpacking tents, radiating outwards like spokes of a wheel, with gas stoves at the hub. Not much of a kitchen, but adequate for heating simple camping ready-meals and pasta, which they would live off for the duration of the trip.

James reached into the large front pocket of his expedition rucksack and with a magician's flourish produced a stack of four grotesque black crow masks. The masks had exaggerated, fierce looking beaks. The other Wednesday Club members looked on with puzzled expressions, Nick shrugged in anticipation, awaiting an explanation.

James; handing out the masks: "Here we go guys, fancy dress for the big event tomorrow night."

Simon: "What the hell are they?"

James: "Venetian masks, which strangely I bought in Prague when I was there with Ann last month. I thought they'd be perfect disguises, that'll bring a sense of irony to our mission. We've targeted this guy for cruelty to innocent creatures. Won't it be great for justice to be dealt out by a bunch of crows?"

The four guys tried on the masks and laughed at the images conjured up in their minds; Buckie being pecked and hounded by six-foot crows. They played few games of poker over their customary whisky "tent warmers" before slithering into their sleeping bags for the long night.

So the Wednesday Club had hatched four avenging crows.

After the chill of the night had been warmed away by their foil bagged breakfasts and hot tea, prepared over propane stoves, the four guys hiked to the remote Druid's Altar. This double-bed sized outcrop of weathered gritstone, topped by a dished horizontal slab, is one of two stones in the Dark Peak said to have been the site of Druid sacrificial offerings to pagan Gods. Its similarly named counterpart, the Druid's Stone, sits high on the plateau of Kinder Scout.

The Druid's Altar would feature in their karma mission that night. This initial visit was necessary to prepare for what would come later.

CHAPTER 9

Karma Delivery

Following their visit to the Druid's Altar, the gang of four Crow Men returned to camp, to fine-tune and rehearse roles for their night's work.

They had been thorough in their preparation: They had each brought along a pair of retired hiking boots that they would be happy to dispose of after the mission. This would ensure that in the event of any detailed investigation, footprints would not lead back to them. They would exchange their regular boots for these old boots on one of the stone slabbed paths that criss-cross the moors, to avoid leaving incriminating trails.

Dressed in their darkest hiking gear, they left camp at 5.30 p.m. As darkness swept across the landscape they headed off towards the shoot's headquarters. Once more they used only starlight and moonlight to light their way.

Conversation was nervously whispered, not because they feared being overheard out on the dark moors, rather that it felt wrong to discuss their imminent adventure in normal voices. None of the Wednesday Club members were accustomed to carrying out this sort of illegal activity. While they were in no doubt that Buckie deserved the treatment they were about to dish out, there was no avoiding the fact that their plans amounted to assault and kidnap.

By 7.15pm they had taken up their rehearsed positions, where, eager and ready for action, they donned their crow mask disguises.

James, Nick and Simon concealed themselves among heather on the edge of a deep peat hag adjacent to the pheasant shoot. Three metres away a dead crow hung limply from the jaws of a pole trap, its wing feathers feebly flapped in the gentle breeze, giving the impression that the bird was attempting to take off for one last flight.

To avoid direct contact with their target, Drew hid in deep heather almost a hundred metres away in an elevated hillside vantage point. Thermal imaging scope by his side, he was the guest spectator for this mission, eager to take in the anticipated drama.

Twenty minutes later James, Simon and Nick spotted Buckie heading their way, shotgun casually slung over his shoulder. As he reached the trap, a callous grin of satisfaction appeared on his face on seeing his grisly trophy dancing in the breeze. Propping his shotgun against the fence, dual barrels pointing to the sky he approached his latest victim.

In an instant, the gamekeeper's world changed from one of smug satisfaction to one of shock, pain and confusion. "What the fuck." He exclaimed as an intense, white light burned into his retinas. In the next moment he was toppled over and pinned to the ground. unable to raise himself more than a few inches, Buckie gasped and struggled beneath what felt like a huge, unbreakable spider's web.

Nick turned off the beam from the powerful, eight hundred lumen LED torch. Buckie's face switched instantly from glowing white to faint grey beneath the coarse nylon net which stretched across his prone body, held tightly in place by James and Simon. Nick then grabbed Buckie's shotgun and broke it open to check whether it was loaded. It was. Turning his back to Buckie, he surreptitiously removed the two cartridges, placing them in his jacket pocket, reclosed the gun, turned and pointed it at the terrified Buckie's face.

Spitting froth from between his yellowed teeth, Buckie exclaimed: "Fucking hell! Who the fuck….What do you want? Do you work for Otto…..Let me up……"

James interrupted Buckie's fearful jabbering: "Shut up and listen. I don't know who the hell Otto is, but we're here to dish up some

47

karma....justice for those defenceless creatures you love to kill and maim."

Buckie: "Ah, now I get it: You're those anti blood sport pricks aren't you. Well you'd better let me go and get the fuck out of here before you're up to your necks in shit deeper than you can even imagine."

Nick kept the gun pointing at Buckie. James knelt on his pounding chest, while Simon held the net in place.

Hiding his nervousness, James snarled his reply: "Almost right, but we're not your average anti blood sports brigade. We're going to take you for a walk across the moor, where we've got a surprise waiting for you."

The three Crow Men dragged Buckie to his feet, wrapping the net around his upper body so that his arms were restrained. Nick positioned himself behind him while Simon and James forced him to stumble forward by dragging him, entangled in the net like an oversized mackerel.

Anger and indignation at his treatment began to overcome Buckie's fear. He raged and threatened the Crow Men. Demanding to know their intentions.

Ignoring Buckie's ranting, James led the way, while Nick and Simon nudged, dragged and prodded Buckie in silence. Drew had hurriedly caught up with them and followed just a couple of metres behind. Four huge crows and a confused gamekeeper entangled in a net. A strange procession worthy of the weirdest carnival. They slowly ascended the hillside, across a snow patched landscape of heather and gurgling streams, to the high moorland location of the Druid's Altar.

Progress was slow and awkward. They crossed half a dozen unavoidable peat hags, these deep waterlogged trenches have steep sides of loose peat that gives way underfoot, causing much slipping and sliding. Once out of the hags, they stumbled and tripped through knee high heather.

When they finally arrived at the Druid's Altar, they nudged Buckie forward, his feet snagging on heather clumps, he stumbled ahead until his chest rested against the cold gritstone slab. A dead crow lay under his nose on top of the ancient altar, head, tail and legs feathered, its torso had been plucked bare.

Buckie: "What the hell's going on?"

James: "Do you know what this rock is?"

Buckie: "Course I do...It's the Druid's Altar."

James: "Do you know what it was used for?"

Buckie: "What the hell are you on about?".

James: "Sacrifices were made on this altar stone. Human sacrifices. That's why we've brought you here.

Buckie's voice trembled: "You're fucking mad, you wouldn't dare...."

James growled: "Shut the fuck up and listen carefully. You now have the choice of two options.
ONE: You can eat that crow, taken from one of your traps, destroy all your traps and stop the killing of wild creatures.
OR
TWO: we sacrifice you here on this stone tonight."

Buckie: "Are you out of your fucking sick minds? I'm not going to eat a crow."

James: "You'd better believe it. We're fucking psychos. We don't give a shit about consequences and we're untouchable. If you choose to survive by taking option one and ever, EVER backslide, we'll come back for you and next time there won't be any options."

Drew: "You sick bastards always fall back on the excuse that you kill to eat. Well here's your chance to prove that. You killed this bird in one of your traps. Enjoy the feast."

Nick and Simon exchanged brief sideways glances at each other, they were both taken aback by the venom with which James had delivered his convincing ultimatum.

James, Simon and Nick crowded around Buckie, in a total invasion of his personal space. Striving to appear as menacing as possible, Nick pressed the shotgun into Buckie's neck.

Simon: "Now Buckie, I suggest you eat your fucking dinner!"

Buckie hesitated then slowly picked up the rotting crow carcass with shaking hands. With a look of revulsion, he tentatively lifted it towards his mouth, holding it an inch from his trembling lips. Nick prodded him with the shotgun again. Buckie responded by nibbling at the crow's plucked breast like a nervous rodent at a roadkill. He gagged and heaved, convulsing involuntarily while trying to swallow rancid morsels of flesh.

Nick and Simon did their best to hide their own queasiness, struggling to supress their own gag reflexes.

After Buckie had forced down five or six mouthfuls of rancid crow flesh, most of which were spontaneously regurgitated, James put an end to the hideous spectacle and without speaking signalled the reluctant diner to move away from the Druid's Altar. Buckie, still restrained by the net, was dragged and pulled until he was once more on the move, tripping and faltering across the rough terrain. It became clear to him that they were now heading back down to the valley, towards his cabins.

The next stage of the mission would be the destruction of all Buckie's traps.

When the strange parade reached steeper ground, Buckie was released from the net to enable him to pick his way down from the high moor without losing his footing. Descending this terrain is more difficult than the ascent and the Crow Men didn't want to risk the inconvenience of Buckie suffering a broken ankle. The shotgun constantly pointing in his direction provided sufficient deterrent against any thought of escape.

Throughout the whole procedure, to avoid any possibility of Buckie recognising his voice from previous encounters, Drew had refrained from talking. He took up a rear-guard position, tagging along behind the returning procession. When they were half a kilometre from the cabins, he peeled away from the group to take up a position where he could once more view the proceedings from a distance, using the night vision scope.

The remaining Crow Men and their captive arrived at a stile where the path left open moorland to enter the woods in which the cabins are located. Buckie begrudgingly led the three remaining Crow Men to the nearest cabin, which housed his small, scruffy office and sleeping quarters. This was the only cabin in complete darkness. Faint light could be seen emanating from the other four cabins, through small gaps around poorly fitted window blinds.

Simon, directing a question to Buckie: "Why are the other cabins lit up?"

Buckie hesitantly stuttered his answer: "Err….Oh…they're the incubators and rearing cages."

On ascending the three wooden steps leading up to the door, Buckie took out his key but found that the door was already unlocked. He assumed that he had inadvertently left it unsecured.

The Crow Men nudged Buckie through the door and followed closely behind him into the cabin's dark interior. Buckie fumbled nervously for the light switch and with a click and flickering of fluorescent lights, the cabin was flooded in harsh, dazzling white light. As their eyes adjusted from night vision mode, to cope with the glare which now filled the cabin, the sight that greeted them shocked them all. Two metres away, across an untidy, pine office table, stood a tall man wearing a menacing scowl, a knife in his left hand and worse; his right hand held a large handgun which was pointing towards the newly arrived group.

CHAPTER 10

A Murder of Crows

"Otto! What are you doing here? I didn't see your car." Buckie gasped.

The interloper, Otto, responded in a thick Dutch accent: "It's a nice night, so I walked up from the road. Anyway, never mind what am I doing here Buckie. What the fuck is going on?"

His gun already pointing in their direction, Otto then turned to the three Crow Men: "You three, take off those stupid masks and slowly put that shotgun down on the floor."

The Crow Men reluctantly removed their sweaty disguises and Nick slowly lowered the shotgun to the floor, all the while maintaining eye contact with Otto.

Buckie nervously jabbered a concise summary of the night's events to Otto, while studying the faces of the Crow Men with contempt in his eyes.

Otto, addressed the Crow Men, pointing towards the scattered chairs: "You idiots are going to wish you'd found another way to amuse yourselves tonight. Shut the door and sit down there."

The Crow Men, still trying to make sense of this alarming development and feeling apprehensive, complied with the order, glancing sideways at each other. Otto moved position to block the path between his seated captives and the door.

Otto then turned to Buckie: "Buckie, pick up your shotgun and if one of these idiots moves, blow his fucking head off. And close those blinds."

Buckie appeared surprisingly underjoyed by this intervention. He clearly wasn't behaving as if he had been rescued from an awkward situation, in fact he appeared to be more uneasy than the Crow Men were. He complied with Otto's instruction, pointing the gun across the table at James, Simon and Nick.

James spoke up cautiously but boldly: "What's this about. Why the weapons?"

From his vantage point in the heather scrub, Drew watched open mouthed as the alarming scene unfolded. The unworldly green imagery produced by the night vision scope had enabled him to see enough through the open door and bare windows, to know that something had gone very wrong. He had to think quickly and act decisively. How could he rescue his friends from this dangerous situation? Just how dangerous he couldn't yet judge. Was this a bluff? A mere show of strength from Buckie's friend or colleague. Or were his mates really in serious danger?

Drew removed his crow mask, hid it in the heather and daubed his face and hands with peaty mud. Pocketing the scope, he ran at a crouch towards the cabin complex. He climbed over a stile in the fence and using the dense bracken that grew abundantly on the site for cover, skirted around the cabin in which his friends were being held. He made his way towards the remaining four cabins. He wondered; did the cabins contain anything he could use? a shotgun maybe? Or did they hide further danger? He had to find out before he could decide on what action to take.

Stooping below window sill level, he crept along the side wall of the first of the cabins. Signs on the four cabin doors indicated that these were pheasant incubating and rearing units and forbade unauthorised access. The windows of all cabins were protected by heavy gauge, galvanised mesh.

Reaching a window with obvious gaps around its closed blind, Drew slowly raised his head until he could see through the narrow gap between the window frame and the blind. As the cabin's interior came into focus, he was astonished to see rows of tall plants growing out of heavy-duty plastic bags. Lines of heat lamps hung from the ceiling. "Shit", he muttered to himself, "this is not good" as he realised that they had unwittingly stumbled across an illegal cannabis growing operation. There was no sign of any occupants in the cabin.

Drew then crept along to the next cabin, taking care to remain out of view. On passing the door, he noticed that a heavy hasp and padlock secured the door. He worked his way around the cabin until he found a window with a lop-sided blind. One side of the blind rested on the antenna of a cheap radio, causing it to slope up at an angle, leaving just enough of a gap to enable him to peer in. He saw movement inside. Two young women were standing at a long work bench, equipped with weighing scales and cutting tools. Faint music could be heard coming from the radio.

The women looked tired and gaunt in the bright artificial light. After watching them for a minute, he realised that they were trimming, weighing and bagging dried cannabis. Beyond the work bench, rows of cannabis plants were hung out to dry on lines of plastic covered wire, which stretched across the cabin. For a moment he watched the drying plants dancing like manic puppets in the artificial breeze produced by rows of fan heaters.

A thought struck Drew; these women are not working here willingly. They're being held captive, otherwise why would the door be locked from the outside? "This is a Cluster Fuck." He muttered under his breath, "Illegal drug manufacturing AND slavery. This whole thing's growing bloody arms and legs."

Drew quickly checked the two remaining cabins. They too were locked from the outside. He was unable to see inside, but after a minute listening against their walls, he was satisfied that they were unoccupied, well by humans at least. No sound whatsoever came from one, from the other he could hear the steady hum of some electrical equipment, sounding like a fridge, along with the occasional chirping of what he assumed were pheasant chicks.

One of these two cabins contained more growing cannabis plants. The other contained a pheasant hatchery, providing a plausible cover story for the presence of heated cabins in such a rural and isolated location. The cannabis farm's remoteness had been the secret of its success. Even in the unlikely event that a police helicopter ever picked up heat sources on its thermal imaging camera, the presence of pheasant incubation units would provide a believable explanation.

The young women Drew had observed, Kristiana and Maria, had been lured to the UK from Moldova on the promise of work and homes. In a sense, this is what they now had, but not in the manner they had been led to expect. Rather than the respectable work, prospects and proper homes they had been promised, they were forced to spend twelve-hour days tending the cannabis plants and preparing the final product for sale on the streets of Manchester. In return all they received were the basics needed to simply exist. Food, clothes and their accommodation. Their living quarters comprised a three metres by four metres room at the rear of Buckie's cabin, containing bunk beds, a TV, sink, table, two chairs and microwave oven. A door from their sparse combined living room and bedroom provided access to a shower room, befitting a nineteen-eighties caravan.

Their Dutch bosses, Otto and his business partner Karl, had transported Kristiana and Maria into the UK via Amsterdam and were holding their passports "for safe keeping."

When the Moldovan women had arrived at the cannabis farm, some six months ago, a Serbian woman, Sonja, was already working here. Kristiana and Maria hadn't become close friends with Sonja, although a mutual respect had developed between them. Sonja always seemed nervous and very reserved, speaking only when necessary.

One day, around three months ago, Sonja failed to return from a shift in the cannabis growing cabins. Otto told the two Moldovan women that Sonja had started to question their instructions, as well as making demands for better working conditions and that her audacity had resulted in a visit to hospital due to an "unfortunate incident". Otto added that she was now being held by UK immigration authorities for contravening entry rules.

Otto and Karl applied the carrot and stick technique to exploit their employees.

The carrot: Kristiana's and Maria's incentive for keeping their heads down, working gruelling hours and enduring grim living conditions, was the promise that they would be released from their servitude after twelve months. They would have their passports returned to them. They would be paid for their labour and would be given papers entitling them to remain in the UK to seek employment. Their labours, they were told, was a fair price for being given this opportunity.

The stick: Fear. Fear of immigration services and fear of violent reprisals. Sonja's disappearance served as a stark reminder of their vulnerability.

Otto was a regular visitor to the cabins, calling at least twice a week to pick up finished product for distribution into his network and to meet with Buckie to check that all was well with the growing and packing operation.

Karl rarely visited, although he was clearly involved with decision making.

The plants they grew were an unusual type, which produced high-potency cannabis. The Dutchmen jealously guarded their strain of plants, referring to them as "our genetics". They had propagated their plants from seeds smuggled in at great risk from California. Their less eloquent street distributors referred to the product as "Otto's top shit".

Drew now had to decide on a course of action. He crept back to the cabin in which his mates were being held and pressed his ear against a wall. He could hear nothing. Keeping one eye closed to maintain night vision, he now risked switching on his head torch to survey the exterior of the cabin. He spotted a thick, black power cable entering the cabin through the wall. Crawling quietly, he traced the cable to its source in the generator housing, where it terminated at a distribution board with switched circuit breakers. Four other cables led from the board, one supply to each cabin.

Drew clicked the switch serving the cable he'd traced from Buckie's cabin to the off position, quickly switched off his head torch and crouching low, hurried back to the far side of the cabin. He was hoping that plunging the cabin into darkness would cause enough confusion to create an opportunity for Simon, Nick and James to escape.

Immediately the lights went out, Drew heard a gunshot and a simultaneous crack as a bullet smashed through a Perspex window, ricocheting of its protective metal grille. He could hear commotion inside the cabin. Otto barked the order to keep still otherwise he'll shoot again. The cabin once more descended into silence. Otto ordered Buckie outside to find out what had happened to the power supply. Drew slithered into the gap below the cabin, between the sloping ground and the floor, concealing himself behind one of the brickwork foundation pads.

Buckie, torch in hand, quickly found the source of the power outage and threw the switch into the ON position bathing the cabin in light once again. On returning to the cabin, he told Otto that the power failure had been the result of an act of sabotage. He had to admit to Otto that he had forgotten to mention the fourth man.

Drew heard Otto, shout at Buckie: "Right, this is a fuck up. You should never have brought these bastards here. I'll get rid of these three, while you find their friend. Take your shotgun and make sure you don't let him get away."

Drew heard Buckie jump down the three steps from the cabin to land heavily on the leaf covered earth. He watched the light from Buckie's torch beam sweep around the bracken and brambles towards the generator hut. Drew cautiously rolled out from below the cabin, quickly rolling back underneath as he heard James, Simon and Nick being noisily marched out through the cabin door in single file. He could see from the feet passing by that Otto followed closely behind. "Make no mistake", Otto barked in his heavy Dutch accent, "If any one of you tries anything, I'll spread your brains all over this fucking place."

The trickle of light that leaked through window blinds, added an artificial yellow patina to the already pale faces of the three captives.

By this time, Otto's mind was in overdrive and he had clearly become unstable. His voice trembled with anger as he spat orders at his prisoners directing them downhill from the cabins. The weak light from the moon and stars was partially cut out by the upper branches of the wintery, leafless trees which cast shadows on the four men, as they followed the convoluted course of a small stream.

Fortunately for Drew, Buckie initially concentrated his search efforts around the generator hut on the opposite side of the complex to his hiding place. Drew once more rolled out from below the cabin and crept the short distance to Buckie's van, taking cover from Otto and Buckie's possible lines of sight.

Drew then stealthily trailed Otto and his friends, crouching low as he crept in the shadows of birch and alder trees. He strained to hear the sounds made by four pairs of feet ahead of him as they pushed through undergrowth, slipping on wet ground and stumbling over exposed tree roots. Long bramble tentacles snagged Drew's trousers, embedding the points of their vicious thorns in his shins, drawing blood as he forced his way through the tangle. His focus remained unflinchingly on the pursuit of his prey.

Buckie widened his search, checking around the cabins, then he headed towards the stile in the fence where he himself was captured earlier in the night. Seeing nothing, he doubled back, heading downhill on the other side of the cabin complex, the sweeping light from his torch illuminating the dried brown bracken and thick undergrowth of tangled brambles. He peered below each cabin before deciding to head off in the direction Otto had taken with his three captives.

Otto instructed the three Crow Men to stop in a clearing. Faint light from the moon and stars illuminated their surroundings. Here the stream they had followed in their forced march from the cabin complex, trickled its contents into an ink-black pond. Like a galactic black hole, any light hitting the pond's surface was swallowed up into its depths.

Pointing the gun at Nick, Otto ordered him to remove two rusty, corrugated metal roofing sheets which lay side by side, covering a section of the pond where it narrowed at its far end. Standing at the margin of the pond, muddy water seeped into Nick's shoes as his feet sank into the soft peat. One at a time, he tilted the metal sheets in order to get a good hold and wrestled them from their wooden railway sleeper supports, which protruded through the surface of the water. The sheets had obviously been there for a while. Dead, brown leaves covered them and winter browned reeds and sedges snagged their rough, rusted edges, tearing away as he pulled to break their hold.

Below the metal sheets Nick saw an outflow, from where the small woodland stream continued its winding, downhill course. The inky black surface of the whole pond was now flecked with silver as the ripples caused by Nick's efforts broke its stillness, to reflect the pale moonlight.

Otto, his voice still shaking with anger, ordered James, Simon and Nick to line up at the edge of the pond, at the point from where Nick had dragged the corrugated sheets. His response to his captives' demands to know what the hell was going on was to aggressively wave his gun towards them and to hold his finger over his lips to indicate that they'd better shut up. Otto's face took on a perplexed frown, as if he was in the process of making a difficult decision.

Keeping low to the ground, Drew had gradually crept within three metres of Otto's position. As he scrutinised Otto in the dim light, he noticed his right hand tighten on the gun and his shoulder and arm stiffen. Otto's hand started to rise. He was clearly intending to shoot his friends.

Drew had run out of thinking time. He had to act immediately if he was to have any chance of saving his mates. He sprang up and launched himself like a charging bull at Otto's back. A metre from Otto, his feet left the ground as he channelled all his strength into a one-chance, flying rugby tackle. On hearing a double click behind him Otto spun around to see Drew mid-flight and Buckie five metres to one side, shotgun raised and puzzled look on his face.

On catching up with Otto, Buckie had spotted Drew a couple of seconds before he desperately jumped into action. On Drew's launch, not realising that he had been carrying around an unloaded weapon, Buckie had raised his shotgun and pulled the trigger. Instead of the explosion of sound and recoil he expected, the gun simply gave a disappointing, empty click.

Time slowed down.

Otto swung his gun towards the airborne Drew and pulled the trigger. A loud crack ripped through the night air.

Otto tumbled backwards carried by the momentum of Drew's flying attack. A spray of blood fanned out from Drew's head, as he landed heavily on top of Otto. Stunned, Buckie and the three remaining Crow Men looked aghast, straining to see the outcome of the explosive burst of action that had just taken place, struggling to convert scrambled thoughts into decisive action.

A split-second after the shot, as if signalled by a starting pistol, James, Simon, Nick and Buckie simultaneously leapt into action. Simon and Nick dashed towards the two heaped bodies, Buckie turned to flee and James charged after Buckie.

Amidst the chaos, Drew could be heard screaming, "Fuckin' hell, I've been shot in the head!"

Simon and Nick arrived simultaneously at Drew's side. Fearing that he had taken a bullet to the head, they were relieved to see that despite the thick splattering of blood matting his hair, the wound on the top of his head appeared superficial. Drew's head had crunched into the underside of the heavy revolver, splitting open his scalp.

Otto, however, had not been so fortunate.

Drew froze for a couple of seconds then with Simon and Nick's assistance, he pushed himself up and off Otto's motionless form, into a kneeling position. He held his hand to the gash on the top of his head and numbly studied the smear of blood that appeared across the base of his thumb. Otto lay motionless, his head twisted to one side and cranked backwards at an unnatural angle, displaying a neat, bloody hole under his chin. Dark liquid oozed out of the top of Otto's head which was cracked open like a hatching egg.

The impact from Drew's head had forced Otto's gun upwards the moment he had pulled the trigger, directing it towards Otto's chin a mere nanosecond before the bullet was expelled from the barrel. In that brief instant, the pendulum of luck had swung in Drew's favour.

With a burst of speed James quickly closed the distance between himself and Buckie, who was trying to run while turning his upper body, in an attempt to point his shotgun at James. James, unsure whether Buckie had managed to reload the gun, jinked from side to side to avoid giving him an easy shot. When he was within reach,

James dove at Buckie, flooring him with a perfect imitation of Drew's rugby tackle which had taken Otto down so effectively.

Stunned brains clicked back into real-time, processing the violence of the past few seconds. Simon, Drew and Nick looked towards James, who by this time had pinned Buckie to the floor, shotgun across his scrawny neck. Satisfied that the threat from Buckie had been neutralised, their attention now fixed on Otto's lifeless form. Feelings of relief, horror and anger came over them.

Relief; that the bullet had missed Drew and that his head wound, caused by the impact with Otto's heavy revolver was clearly not life threatening.

Horror; that a man lay dead in their midst. An evil bastard, who had intended to kill them, but still a human being.

Anger; at Buckie, who had clearly intended to kill Drew and James. Had Nick not removed the cartridges from Buckie's shotgun, their situation would certainly have been much worse.

The Wednesday Club members now had blood on their hands.

CHAPTER 11

Shit Creek, Shortage of Paddles

Nick produced the two shotgun cartridges from his pocket and with an uncharacteristic, sneering grin, stood over Buckie and shook them angrily at arms-length towards his face. No words were needed, Buckie, still pinned down by James, realised that Nick had unloaded his shotgun. He reacted with a blank, dead-fish expression and with a stifled shrug, whimpered shakily: "Well, what happens now?"

James muttered under his breath: "Need to think. Need to think carefully."

Drew, switching on his headtorch: "We're right up Shit Creek. What do we do now? Call the police?"

James: "No mate, we're in too deep to hope we'll come out of this smelling of roses if we involve the police."

James then turned to Buckie, growling assertively: "Right! Get up Buckie."

Buckie understood from the tone of James's voice that he was in no position to negotiate. He obligingly stood up, bottom lip trembling and arms hanging limply by his side like a schoolboy that had just lost a playground fight.

James held his hand out towards Nick, who without the need for words, knew exactly what James wanted. He handed over the two shotgun cartridges, which James promptly loaded into the twin barrels of Buckie's gun.

James pointed the shotgun at Buckie's head and told the others to stand well back. Buckie buckled at the knees, pissed himself and wailed like a frightened pup. He begged James not to kill him. He promised to do anything they wanted and swore that he would never reveal what had happened here tonight.

Simon, Drew and Nick looked on, anticipating James's next move. Backing away slowly, they were transfixed and horrified by the surreal scene unfolding before them.

James lowered the gun's aim to Buckie's chest and then ordered him to drag Otto's body to the edge of the pond, where a minute earlier Nick, Simon and James had stood, awaiting execution at Otto's hands.

Buckie complied, straining with the dead weight of the big Dutchman, he heaved Otto's limp body through the mud and let him drop face down in the thick mat of reeds that bordered the edge of the pond. Buckie eyeballed the handgun that was still held in Otto's dead grip. In response, James twitched the shotgun at Buckie and gave him a look that he clearly understood. Don't even think about it!

James addressed Buckie: "This is what happens now if you want to see another day: You slowly take the gun from your dead friend's hand, and keep the barrel pointing towards the floor. No tricks. I bet I could unload both barrels of this thing into you before you could even lift that gun."

Buckie did as he had been instructed. "What now?"

James pointing to the ground about a metre from Otto's body: "Ok, stand here, hold the gun at arm's length, aim it at Otto's back and pull the trigger. Make sure you hit him in the shoulder blade"

A look of incredulity came over Buckie's pale, scowling face as he started to protest. James halted Buckie's objection with a jab of the shotgun. No words were needed. Simon, Nick and Drew all instinctively held their arms across their faces and stepped backwards. Buckie obeyed James's instruction and Otto's body bucked with the impact of the shot.

James, directed another order at Buckie: "Now turn him over."

Buckie recoiled: "Why?"

James: "I want to make sure the bullet is still inside his body."

Buckie grasped Otto's jacket at the shoulder with one hand and his gripped the leg of his jeans with the other, then clumsily rolled him onto his back. There was no exit hole visible in his front. Satisfied with the result, James moved onto the next stage of the damage mitigation exercise. He asked Nick to hurry back to the open cabin to find a plastic bag. He did so without question, quickly returning with a supermarket bag that had been lining the office bin.

Still pointing the shotgun towards Buckie, James ordered him to search Otto's pockets. Buckie removed a tatty leather wallet bulging with cash. No doubt the proceeds from recent drug sales.

James: "Count the money."

Buckie did as he was told and announced that there was sixteen hundred and forty pounds. James told a bewildered Buckie to put the money in his own pocket.

James: "You're not keeping it. You're going to give half each to the women in the cabin."

James then told Buckie to remove the bullets from the gun and to drop the gun and bullets into the bag. Buckie, now resigned to obeying orders unquestioningly, did as he'd been instructed.

James: "Ok Buckie. You can now get out of this alive. We're going to store this gun somewhere safe as our insurance policy. Its got your fingerprints all over it and one of its bullets inside Otto. If you breathe a word to anyone that implicates any of us, the gun will end up with the police and you'll end up in prison, watching your arse every time you have a shower for the next twenty years."

Buckie: "What about Karl?"

James: "Who's Karl?"

Buckie enlightened the Crow Men regarding Karl's role in the cannabis farming enterprise.

In the confusion of the past few minutes, none of the Crow Men had noticed Buckie casting puzzled glances at Drew each time he spoke. Buckie's mind was grinding away in an effort to place the familiar voice.

Drew shone his headlamp into the dark water of the pond at the point where Otto had clearly intended to dump his mates' bodies. They ordered Buckie to slide Otto's body into the water and to replace the corrugated metal roofing sheets to cover the pond's gruesome secret.

As Buckie was struggling to push, pull and heave Otto's heavy frame into the water, Drew pointed silently at the pond where the light from the headlamp played. He exclaimed "Shit! what the fuck is that?" They all peered into the murky water. A metre below the surface a hideous green creature was writhing around among two rows of curved yellowed twigs. As they gawped at the spectacle, two long, fat eels thrashed explosively from the twigs, disappearing into the pond's darker depths to take cover from the light. When the ripples settled, a pale, yellow ball-like object came into view, bobbing up towards the surface. Disturbed by the eels' rapid departure, it rolled to one side revealing black, empty eye sockets and a skeletal grin. A human skull. Drew and Buckie jumped back, startled by their grim discovery. It now dawned on them that those other objects weren't twigs, they were ribs. There was a human skeleton in the pond.

"My God. "Sonja!" Gasped Buckie. "I knew they were lying about her disappearance."

Nick: "Sonja. Who the hell is Sonja?"

Buckie, clearly horrified by the gruesome discovery, went on to explain about Sonja's brief career at the cannabis farm. He omitted to mention that during their shared time there, he and Sonja had grown close. Close enough for Buckie to convince himself that something more than friendship might be on the horizon. He had been devastated when Sonja disappeared from his life.

The Crow Men believed Buckie when he claimed he hadn't known that she had been killed and dumped in this lonely grave, so far from her Serbian home. Buckie's shock and dismay was almost palpable. An Oscar winning actor couldn't have put on a more convincing display.

Buckie, being aware that both Otto and Karl were capable of callous brutality, realised that Sonja's disappearance had been far more sinister than he had been led to believe. It was now apparent to him that Otto's claim that she had been arrested by the authorities had been a cover story.

The Crow Men allowed Buckie to pause in his efforts to despatch Otto's body into the pond. As he tried to compose himself, he explained that he himself had introduced eels into the pond a couple of years ago, to dispose of the corpses of unwanted pheasants, which the shooters would triumphantly carry back to the cabins only to change their minds about taking them home to eat.

The eels were obviously capable of scavenging much bigger carrion. They had grown fat from their grisly feast.

Buckie was pressed into completing his task of sinking Otto's corpse in the eel pond. He received no assistance from the Crow Men who kept their distance to avoid the risk of leaving minute traces of their presence on the body. They had seen enough detective films and CSI TV episodes to make them healthily obsessed in that respect.

When Buckie had finally heaved Otto's corpse into the water, he covered the narrow end of the pond, using the metal sheets that had been used to conceal Sonja's remains. Once more darkness descended on the eels feasting place, inviting the slimy scavengers to return and put their needle-sharp teeth to use.

There was a sense of ironic justice in the choice of Otto's resting place. It was he, not Karl that had killed Sonja.

The effort needed to consign Otto to his murky grave took its toll on Buckie. He crouched on his haunches wheezing. When his breathing had calmed and his face had lost its purple hue, the Crow Men instructed him on what he must do next. Despite their enmity, they were all in a deep hole together and their only chance of extracting themselves from the hole would be through a collaborative effort. The four Wednesday Club members would ensure that most of the effort and the risk would land squarely on Buckie's shoulders.

Keeping a wary eye, and the shotgun, trained on Buckie; James, Simon, Nick and Drew held an impromptu, whispered conflab. They had to hastily decide on a course of action that would play out over the next few hours and days, the consequences of which would hang over them for the remainder of their lives.

Having hurriedly considered every angle and implication they could think of in the short time available, they concocted a multi-layered plan in which Buckie would play a central role.

Buckie was to contact Karl to relay a concocted story, designed to keep Karl at arm's length from the truth. Before contacting Karl, he was to clear out all traces of the drug operation from the site.

The fabricated story that Buckie had to memorise, rehearse and then convincingly deliver to Karl would be that;
Otto had been to see Buckie in a panic to tell him that the cannabis farm had been compromised. He had seen two people snooping around the cabins that he recognised as distributors of their product, they were key members of their Manchester supply chain. Now their secret location was no longer a secret it would only be a matter of

69

time before other drug gangs would get to hear of it. The security of their precious genetics was in jeopardy. This was a risk Otto couldn't take, so he had instructed Buckie to dismantle the operation and to "sanitise" the cabins to remove all traces of their business. The Moldovan women were to be put on a train to London and told they were free, but it must be made very clear to them that if they ever spoke a word about the cannabis farm to anyone, there would be a hefty price to pay. Buckie had neither seen nor heard from Otto since.

James: "Uncomfortable I know Buckie, but unless you have a better suggestion….?"

Buckie, his mind ticking over: "No."

James: "Well at least one part of the story will be true."

Buckie gave James a puzzled look. Despite his obvious wariness and mistrust of these new, unwelcome acquaintances, who had burst uninvited into his World and, in the space of one night, torn it apart, he realised that they were all now definitely up the same Shit Creek, suffering from a serious lack of paddles.

Buckie didn't exactly feel relaxed in the company of James, Simon, Nick and Drew, but he realised that he wasn't dealing with the sheer ruthlessness and brutality which is inherent in the world of drug gangs and dealers. He perceived a sense of reason and justice pervading their actions.

The next part of the plan entailed dealing with the problem of the Moldovan women. James instructed Buckie that he was to unlock the cabin in which Kristiana and Maria were incarcerated and to speak with them. He had to hand Otto's money to them and let them know that their enslavement was over. He was then to transport them to Piccadilly Station in the centre of Manchester, where they would be free to board a train to wherever they wish, so long as they did not return to Manchester. They felt they could be confident of their silence, as any discussion with the authorities would expose them as illegal immigrants. Also, while they had probably heard some of the night's violent events, they couldn't possibly have seen anything of them.

James. "Here's what you're going to do. And just to remind you, there's a corpse in that pond with your name on it. If you drop the ball….well….. I'm sure you wouldn't want either the police or Otto's drug dealer mates to find out about that, would you?

Get the women into the back of your van and lock them in. Then drive them to Piccadilly station. Drop them along Store Street at a point where its unlikely there'll be any CCTV cameras. Point them towards the station and then get your arse back here.

By the time you return, we'll have gone. Just remember that we'll be watching you over the next week or two, while you get rid of every sign of the cannabis farm and make these cabins look like what it says on the tin…pheasant rearing huts."

James, now directing his comment to everyone: "This shit is unreal, and deep. The only way we'll get out of it unscathed, relatively speaking, is if we all pull together."

Buckie: "You don't want much from me do you?"

James: "This is the only option for you Buckie. It's the only way you have a chance of walking the streets a free man. We'll give you two weeks from today and then we'll blow the whistle."

Buckie: "What! I thought…."

James: "Wait Buckie and listen. We'll blow the whistle, but not on you. One of us will anonymously phone the cops to say we were walking the dog, peeked under the corrugated sheets and to our shock and horror…..you can guess the rest. We then have to hope that the police reach the conclusion that the killings were drug-gang related, which they are really, and the reason the bodies were found in this remote location is that it was a simply a handy, isolated spot to dispose of their burden. Nothing to do with your pheasant murdering work."

"So Buckie, you have two weeks in which to get rid of anything that might hint at the existence of the cannabis farm you have been running here and to make it look as though it has never been anything but a legit pheasant rearing facility. You've got a big cleaning job ahead of you".

Buckie: "Why not just leave the bodies? They might never be found. That's just asking for trouble."

James: "One: because they will be found at some time, and better to face this at a time when you are switched on and prepared, than be caught unawares in ten years' time.
And two: Because somewhere in Serbia, there's a family wondering whatever happened to their loved one; Sonja. This way, if the police do their job properly, they might just get an answer to their nightmare."

Simon, with a glimmer of hope entering his mind for the first time since Otto's brutal demise: "Also if they connect Sonja to people trafficking, that'll divert attention towards organised crime rather than gamekeepers and hikers."

Buckie made his way to the main cabin to collect the key to the padlock, which secured the drug drying and packing cabin. The Moldovan women had been locked in there for the duration of their shift.

James: "A question Buckie; just out of interest. What came first, the cannabis growing career or gamekeeping?"

Buckie: "Gamekeeping. I was pressured into the drug thing by Otto and Karl. They somehow picked the shoot out as the ideal cover for their business and made a very uncomfortable and scary visit to me one night while I was here at the cabin. Believe me, I wasn't given a choice in this. Yes, I could have gone to the police, but Karl pulled a picture of my daughter out of his wallet. There was no doubt what was meant by that. These bastards are ruthless."

The four Crow Men quietly reflected on Buckie's revelation. Despite their differences over Buckie's chosen career, they couldn't help but feel some pity for the desperate no-win situation that the Dutch drug dealers had forced upon him.

Wanting to avoid face to face contact with the Moldovan women, the four Wednesday Club guys made their way up to Drew's earlier vantage point, where they could check on Buckie's progress concealed by the night and the terrain. On their way out of the cabin complex, Simon, Nick and James collected their crow masks from the table, leaving Drew to collect his from the mud at their hiding place.

In whispered conversation, while taking turns with the night vision scope to spy on Buckie's activities around the cabins, the Crow Men shared and aired their thoughts and feelings on what they had just been through.

The overriding emotion shared by all four was guilt; Otto was dead because of them. They would need to deal with this troubling thought over the coming months. Key to their self-administered therapy was the mantra that there was now one less evil, murdering scumbag in the World. They would also remind each other that they hadn't actually killed him, Otto had pulled the trigger himself in an attempt to kill Drew. Not quite suicide, but neither was it murder. They chose to label his death as self-inflicted misadventure.

They also felt guilt at not assisting the Moldovan women more. Their options had been limited, as keeping a distance was imperative to their concealment. At least the women were now free and safe from Otto and Karl.

Their second concern, a close second to guilt, was of course the fear of being implicated in the death of Otto. Their hope on that score, was that by the time the police investigate, the eels and two weeks of Dark Peak winter weather, will have significantly removed any evidential traces that might lead to them. All four had kept their gloves on throughout, so no finger prints had been left behind. The gloves would soon be joining their boots on a trip to the bottom of a very deep reservoir. The most worrying remnant of their presence was the blood from Drew's head wound, but they had ordered Buckie to douse the area near the pond with buckets of water until there was no trace of blood to be seen.

CHAPTER 12

The Dutchmen

In the late 1990s Otto and Karl had both dropped out of their courses at the University of Amsterdam and travelled together to Humboldt County, a remote part of California that attracts new-age travellers, hippies and adventurers looking for an "off-grid" haven.

Due to its climate, remoteness and the difficulty of enforcing the law in such a remote and wild area, Humboldt is home to many illegal cannabis farms and is drug-world-famous as the source of highly sought after strains of the plant, renowned for their high potency and hence high street value.

Otto and Karl had easily found low-paid work on an isolated cannabis farm, located two hours by road from the nearest town. The farm was owned by a rough and ignorant man in his late fifties and his two twenty-something year old sons, who were rumoured to be the product of separate incestuous relationships. The sons' mothers had long since left, bored and disillusioned by the loneliness and crudeness of life on the farm. Otto and Karl often joked with each other about the sons' odd features and referred to them as the six-fingered banjo boys.

Karl and Otto's hopes of a rapid road to riches were short-lived. Work was hard, with long hours and primitive conditions. Their living quarters was a moss-covered 1970s mobile home. Pay, when they received it, was an insulting pittance. Their only entertainment was satellite TV and alcohol, mostly rough spirit they had distilled themselves using whatever grain or starchy vegetables they could lay their hands on.

For much of the time, Otto and Karl were high from the effects of alcohol or the crop they were employed to farm.

After enduring these unrelenting slave-like conditions for eight months, while drunk on a fresh and particularly potent batch of their homemade moonshine, Karl and Otto made a spur of the moment decision to take revenge on their employers and to relieve them of their cash. From their sneakily made observations, they knew that the proceeds of the family's drug sales were hidden in a locked, steel box under the floor of the barn, above which their employer's beaten-up pickup truck was usually parked.

One night, around 3 a.m. they quietly barricaded the two outward opening external doors of the house by wedging them with logs from the woodpile. They then poured petrol around the whole perimeter of the timber-built house, taking care to thoroughly douse all doors and windows. They then ignited the petrol-soaked house and threw an open can of petrol through a window, tossing lighted petrol-soaked rags after it.

The resulting conflagration was explosive, the intense fire consumed all the oxygen inside the house in seconds. The occupants didn't have any chance of escape and they perished almost instantly from inhalation of hot gases.

Otto and Karl stood coldly and calmly listening to the brief, dying screams of the drug farmer and his sons. They watched the total destruction of the house in awe, feeling an overwhelming sense of power and invulnerability. This callous act represented an escalation in the level of ruthless punishment they were prepared to inflict on anyone that stood in their way.

As the farm was so remote, they knew it was unlikely that the fire would be seen. They took their time, rooting out the cash box from its hiding place, smashing open the lock with a lump hammer and spade. They collected the five packets of seeds that had been harvested from last year's cannabis crop and stored in the barn with the cash. These seeds were to be the foundation of their future. From them, they would grow their own crops and make their fortune. All they had to do now was to leave the country, head back to The Netherlands and start up their own growing operation. Simple.

Otto and Karl managed to leave the USA before the tragic fire at their previous employer's home was discovered. They were confident that there would be no trail leading from the crime to them. Clearly no records of employees were kept in the illicit cannabis business. They hoped that the overstretched law agencies would attribute the fire to rival growers. The farm had been a small scale operation, which often came under pressure from larger competing enterprises in the region.

They used the horticultural skills and knowledge they had gained in Humboldt to set up small scale growing operations close to Amsterdam and Rotterdam, using space leased from cooperative bulb and flower farmers. The reputation of their high quality, stolen strain of plant soon grew, as did the demand for it. Drug dealers from the UK showed an interest in setting up a distribution chain for their "genetics" as Otto and Karl referred to their strain of plants.

Transporting their product to the UK entailed significant risk. The UK coastguard, border and security agencies were ever vigilant and twice their carriers had been intercepted and arrested at ferry ports.

Always entrepreneurs, Karl and Otto decided that in order to reduce the risk of shipping product to the UK, they would set up a growing operation here. After much thought, they settled on the peculiar choice of game bird shoots as a target location for growing their plants, fulfilling their requirements with regard to remoteness, concealment and cover.

As Manchester was one of their biggest markets, they looked for a suitable site within easy reach of the city. After a month spent researching potential sites, they homed in on the Hindhurst shoot. It's isolation and apparent lax management being clinching features.

Two weeks after taking that decision, they burst uninvited into Buckie's life and ensnared him as a reluctant partner.

After their murderous exit from the drug scene in the USA, strong-arming a simple minded gamekeeper into cooperating with them was mere child's play.

Otto and Karl had acted on drunken impulse when they had wreaked havoc at the Humboldt cannabis farm. Reflecting back on that incident, they realised just how dangerously reckless their actions had been and that their escape from justice had been down to luck. They made a resolution that meticulous planning would be the cornerstone of their future business strategy.

Initially Buckie resisted their approach, but his refusal to cooperate brought threats of violence to himself and to his daughter resulting in his immediate capitulation.

CHAPTER 13

My Enemy's Enemy

Over the week following Otto's death, motivated by his well-developed sense of self-preservation, Buckie took his task of dismantling and removing all traces of the now defunct cannabis farm seriously. He scrubbed, burned or buried all traces of the operation, from plant seeds to finished, packaged product. Not one to miss an opportunity to profit, Buckie hid the packaged cannabis and seeds in the base of a dry-stone wall in a remote part of the shoot. He carefully wiped all packaging to remove any traces or fingerprints that in the unlikely event it was found, might point to him.

After clearing the site of all traces of the drug growing and packaging operation, Buckie then populated all the cabins with pheasant rearing paraphernalia. Most of this effort had been completed within the first frantic week.

The Moldovan women were now off the scene. They had never been allowed to see outside their tiny, confined world for duration of their labours for Otto and Karl. They hadn't even known what part of the UK they were in, so they weren't considered a risk. No doubt their efforts would now be entirely concentrated on the future. They would realise that any revelation of their recent past would put them under an unwelcome microscope.

A week before James's call would be made to the police, Buckie had almost completed his sanitisation of the site. At the end of a particularly long and difficult day, an uninvited late-night caller visited Buckie's home.

Karl knocked loudly on the door of Buckie's tiny rented terraced cottage, situated on the outskirts of Hindhurst. He didn't wait to be invited in. Immediately the door cracked open, Karl heaved his significant bulk against it, forcing Buckie back into the entrance hall, almost knocking him off his feet. Buckie steadied himself against the wall and grumbled a protest, but Karl simply frog-marched him into the living room and pushed him down on the nearest chair.

Karl stood over Buckie and demanded to know what was going on. For four days, he had tried to contact Otto without any success. Then he had visited the cannabis farm site in darkness. On receiving no response to knocks hammered on the doors of the unlit living quarters, office and drying and packing cabins, he had kicked in their doors. Discovering that the site had been deserted and cleared, he decided to make his house call on Buckie.

Buckie had been caught off guard. He stammered and stuttered incoherently while mustering his thoughts. He faked a coughing fit until Karl allowed him to get himself a glass of water. His delay tactics bought him a valuable extra minute, giving him the time he needed to bring to mind the fabricated story, which the Wednesday Club members had imprinted in his mind.

Buckie carefully relayed the invented and much rehearsed story to Karl, who stood over him, glaring impassively until he had finished.

Karl scowled and snarled his response at Buckie: "That whole story stinks like bullshit man. Otto would have contacted me immediately if he thought we had problems. He wouldn't just panic into clearing the site without first discussing it. Something's badly wrong here."

Karl started to lose his temper. It occurred to him that he was being cheated. But by whom? Otto? Buckie? He really didn't believe that Buckie had either the ambition or the balls to cross him. On the other hand, Otto was his long-standing partner in crime, surely he wouldn't double cross him.

Dirty plates bounced and cutlery skittered as Karl thumped his fist down hard on the dining table. He demanded to know where the finished product and the seeds for their precious "genetics" were.

Buckie feigned ignorance and stuck to his story. He didn't dare add his own embellishments. He was stuck between the devil and the deep blue. His only unrehearsed addition was to suggest that Otto might have stashed the product and seeds away safely until they could set up elsewhere.

Frustrated and angry, Karl stormed from the house, slamming the door behind him so hard that draughty old sash windows, front and back, rattled in their frames. His next task would be to search for Otto.

To avoid any direct contact with the police, James's whistle-blow call was made to the local Mountain Rescue team. He used their enquiries number, as emergency calls to Mountain Rescue are handled by police 999 operators.

Finding a functioning public telephone these days isn't easy. Fortunately, there are still a few around, mainly in isolated locations where mobile phone signals are sparse. On finding a suitably remote phone box, James parked almost a kilometre away and walked as inconspicuously as possible to the weather-worn, red box. Before ducking inside to make the call, he scanned the area to make sure no one was around. He dialled with gloved hands and used the 141 prefix to conceal the source of the call.

On the fourth ring, the call was answered. James effected a precautionary, low pitch disguise to his voice, while doing his best imitation of a Yorkshire accent. He relayed anonymously to the Mountain Rescue volunteer a fabricated story that, while walking his dog in the woods, he had stumbled upon a body in a pond. He quickly gave map coordinates for the location and ignoring pleas for more details, ended the call and hurried away from the phone box.

CHAPTER 14

The Bombshell

The call from James kick-started a whole chain of frenetic police activity. Two bodies were quickly found. The whole area was taped off, controlled as a crime scene and placed under twenty-four hour guard.

Anyone not involved in the police investigation was excluded from the area. An exception was made for a supervised visit by Buckie, who, for animal welfare reasons, had been allowed to remove his stock of pheasant chicks to a temporary location.

The police fruitlessly searched the surrounding area for further bodies and evidence.

Very little information from the police investigation reached public domain. Generalised summaries were released to the press, simply indicating that two bodies had been discovered under suspicious circumstances.

The owners of the shooting estate had been questioned. They had referred the police to Buckie who was then interviewed in his home by the police. He feigned shock on hearing of the grisly discovery made in the eel pond and promised to rack his brains in an attempt to recall anything that might be significant to the investigation. When questioned about the recent damage to the cabin doors, he pointed the finger of blame at "the antis" referring to anti blood sports activists.

Two days after James's call to Mountain Rescue, Karl had revisited the site hoping to shed light on what had happened. Seeing the police activity, he made a hasty retreat followed by another late-night visit to Buckie.

This time, Karl didn't bother to knock on the front door to announce his arrival. He skulked down the narrow back street which runs behind the row of seven stone-built cottages and locating Buckie's back yard clambered over the solid wooden gate. He was instantly greeted by frantic barking of dogs. Buckie kept his working spaniel and two terriers in a range of kennels and runs which occupied the whole length of his yard. Karl was unfazed by the commotion, he dashed to the back door and pressed himself into the shadowy recess of the doorway. A scruffy, make-shift porch roof screened him from the view of anyone looking through upstairs windows. Karl remained statue-still.

Buckie slept in the front bedroom of the cottage. On being woken by his dogs, he rubbed his eyes, leapt out of bed and stumbled into the rear bedroom. He opened the window and surveyed the yard. Seeing nothing out of order, he assumed that one of the neighbours cats had wandered into his yard. The dogs, still aware of Karl's presence continued to bark despite Buckie's protests.

Karl heard the upstairs window close. He moved quickly to the kitchen window and slid the four-inch blade of his lock-knife into the horizontal slot between the two frames of the sash window. The simple, old security catch was easily nudged aside, allowing Karl to raise the lower section of the window. By the time Karl had clambered through the open window and clumsily extricated himself from the inconveniently positioned Belfast sink, Buckie had reached the door into the kitchen.

Karl was on Buckie in a split second, pinning him to the wall, pressing his thick forearm into his Adam's apple and pointing the blade of his knife towards his right eye.

Buckie froze, not daring to move.

Karl demanded to know why the police were at the site of his cannabis farm.

Buckie, terrified by Karl's violent invasion of his home, crumbled under the pressure of this second inquisition. He told Karl that he had heard about two bodies being discovered, adding that he wondered if one of them might be Otto. Buckie, keeping to the script he had agreed with the four guys who were now pulling his strings, suggested to Karl that maybe a rival drug gang had been responsible.

To deflect Karl's anger and to add credibility to his own story, Buckie claimed that, not realising Otto was dead, he had given the packaged drugs to a friend, who had agreed to store it safely until Otto reappeared.

Karl: "Why did you tell me you didn't know where the drugs were when I asked you? You lied to me and that's not good for your health."

Buckie: "I thought I was doing the right thing for Otto and that he would sort it all out with you when he got back. But now it seems that he won't be coming back."

Sceptical of Buckie's explanation, Karl pressed him to reveal details of the friend who was holding the drugs. Buckie unhesitatingly put Drew in the frame. After all, if it hadn't been for Drew's interference, he wouldn't be in this predicament.

Later that week, on the evening of the day of Drew's routine visit to the nature reserve, Buckie waited in his van at the Lamb Inn car park. Drew's routine ran like clockwork. He habitually visited the Lamb for a beer at the end of his shift, then he would usually move on to the Greenman for a meal and a coffee.

After Drew had parked his car in the car park at the rear of the pub, Buckie hung back giving Drew time to buy his usual pint and find a seat, before following him into the pub lounge. He then furtively entered the pub and sat down across from Drew, hands clasped in his lap, a sheepish look on his face.

Drew raised his eyebrows, casting a puzzled look across the table towards Buckie. After a couple of stuttering false starts, Buckie explained in a whisper, that despite Drew having plastered his face with mud on the night of the confrontation which had resulted in Otto's death, he had recognised him. Then, dropping the bombshell, he told Drew about Karl's latest visit and nervously explained that he had had no choice other than to drag Drew back into the thick of it, centre stage in fact.

Attempting to excuse his duplicity, Buckie explained that Karl had threatened and intimidated him. Adding that had he admitted to Karl that he had squirrelled away the cannabis himself, he probably wouldn't be alive now. He had acted out of self preservation.

Drew, tried to contain his anger, overcoming the urge to yell at Buckie: "Well thanks for that. I ought to punch you in the face right here and now."

Buckie: "Sorry. I had no choice. I really need your help if I'm going to get out of this in one piece. I did help you cover up….you know what. And; don't forget that it was your attack on me that set this whole thing in motion"

Buckie explained that he had promised Karl he would get Drew to return the drugs and in return Karl had agreed to leave them both in peace once that transaction was complete.

Drew's mind was working overtime, trying to figure out what he could do to extract himself from this ongoing nightmare?

Drew got up to leave, hesitating as Buckie begged him to stay while they figure out together the best course of action, he reluctantly returned to his chair.

After a heated but hushed discussion, Drew suggested an approach which they agreed on: Buckie would contact Karl and tell him that

Drew had stashed the cannabis in a crag high on Bleaklow Moor. Buckie would bring Karl to a meeting point close to the hiding place, from where Drew would lead them to the drugs. The meeting would be set for three days' time, allowing two days for preparation.

Drew's hope was that Karl would stick to his word and simply walk away with the product. However, he needed a contingency plan in place, that would keep him, and Buckie, safe in the event Karl decided to play things differently.

Having agreed the meeting time and place, Drew, his mind still reeling from this new development, swiftly exited the Lamb Inn, leaving his pint of beer unfinished on the table. He immediately phoned James from his car, informed him of what had just transpired and requested that the other three Wednesday Club members meet him urgently, to discuss this whole mess.

This was a strange and paradoxical twist to the circumstances and events that had brought them to this point. Drew and Buckie were now having to work together, for their very survival. My enemy's enemy is my friend. Well not exactly friends in this case, but collaborators.

Buckie reached across the table, picking up Drew's abandoned beer, which he unashamedly knocked back. He then ordered another. Dutch courage to help him deal with a dangerous Dutch adversary. He intended to call Karl as soon as he arrived home, to propose the arrangements for handing over the product, which he had just agreed with Drew.

As Drew drove from the car park, he noticed a pale face peering towards him from a silver hatchback car parked next to the exit. The occupant's dazzled eyes squinted in the glare from Drew's headlights. Under normal circumstances he wouldn't have given this a second thought, but in the current situation Drew was unnerved. This person was clearly intent on getting a good look at him. Was this Karl? Was Buckie playing games? Were the police watching him?

Karl was mistrusting by nature. In his line of work this trait had been key to staying in business and staying out of prison for twenty years. Under present circumstances his mistrust had escalated into full-blown paranoia. Karl had been following Buckie around since his phone call. He had trailed him to the pub and peering through the glass panels in the door, had observed Buckie's fraught meeting with Drew.

Karl didn't like loose ends, he needed to find out who Buckie had been speaking to and why, so he returned to his car and waited. When Buckie left the pub, Karl hurried across the car park, intercepting him as he unlocked his van. Karl forced Buckie to shuffle around the gear stick, across to the passenger side, enabling Karl to climb into the driver's seat. Leaning across, towards Buckie, Karl demanded to know who? what? and why? Buckie decided that at that point, honesty, partial at least, would be the best policy. His mind, dulled by beer, wasn't switched on sufficiently to conjure up a convincing alternative. He told Karl that he had just met with Drew to talk him into handing over the cannabis and to arrange for him to meet Karl at the place where it was hidden.

Buckie gave Karl the proposed meeting arrangements he and Drew had agreed upon earlier that evening.

Karl initially refused to go along with the suggested meeting time and location, insisting that Buckie and Drew should bring the drugs to him at his own choice of location. Buckie informed Karl that Drew point-blank refuses to handle the drugs any further, due to events having escalated far beyond his comfort zone. Perhaps emboldened by alcohol, Buckie was uncharacteristically forceful in playing the ace he felt he had up his sleeve. He insisted that if Karl wanted the product, the only option would be to meet at the location the drugs were already hidden, in accordance with the arrangements Drew was insisting on for the handover.

After some rumination, Karl reluctantly agreed to meet Drew on Bleaklow for the pick-up.

Karl wanted some insurance in place. He toned down his anger and subtly extracted from Buckie as much background information on Drew as he could.

Buckie's next task was to retrieve the drugs from his hiding place in the dry-stone wall on the pheasant shoot and hand them over to Drew for concealment at the place chosen for the handover meeting with Karl. Feeling wary after Karl's unexpected appearance outside the Lamb Inn, he took extra care to ensure he wasn't followed. He circled Hindhurst's small roads in his van, doubling back a couple of times before heading off. After collecting the drugs he met Drew in the carpark of a twenty four hour supermarket, close to Drew's house.

Immediately after Buckie had made his delivery, Drew made a lone, night-time trip out on Bleaklow Moor where he concealed the drugs in a deep cleft in a gritstone crag. He then drove back to his own house to meet his three Wednesday Club mates for the impromptu meeting he had requested.

Drew outlined the recent turn of events to the others. His problem was immediately acknowledged as being a mutual problem, to be shared and solved by all four. They had to protect Drew and they had little time to consider their best course of action.

The drug handover meeting time and location was cast in stone, unmovable. It had been difficult to get Karl's agreement and any change would certainly be unacceptable to Karl.

Fuelled by strong coffee, the four friends devised a plan to provide back-up to Drew. From Drew's conversation with Buckie, they realised that Karl was unstable and dangerous and while they hoped the handover would be straightforward and drama free, they concluded that they had to be prepared to fight fire with fire if events turned dangerous.

Their plan entailed James, Simon and Nick concealing themselves around the crag, close to the meeting location, to observe the handover. The abundance of huge gritstone boulders and rock formations in the immediate vicinity of the crag would offer plenty options for concealment. Their main concern was how they could intervene with sufficient speed if the unpredictable Karl turned violent. From their encounter with Otto they expected that Karl would also be armed.

They discussed the possibility of carrying Otto's gun to the meeting, but this was soon discounted as none of them was competent enough with firearms. Also the risk to themselves due to inaccurate shooting or panic was too high. Eventually they decided that their deadly force capability would have to be provided by James's competition longbow. James was confident and highly accurate with this familiar weapon.

Drew's meeting with Karl had been set for 10.00 p.m.

On the evening of the meeting, guided by Drew in the chill of a February night, all four made their way on to Bleaklow. Winter walking on the high moors can be seriously cold, but hanging around motionless, as they planned to do for some time that night, was just inviting hypothermia to strike. They hiked up to the remote part of the moor wearing and carrying full winter gear as protection against the windchill of a brisk north easterly wind.

Drew pointed out the location of the stashed cannabis; a dark, moss lined cleft at the base of the crag.

Faces blackened and striped commando style with mud, Simon, James and Nick were in position by 7.30 p.m. each concealed in vantage points surrounding the crag. They were invisible to Karl and Buckie's approach route, but positioned close enough to observe the transaction taking place, even in the black of the night.

Half an hour before the appointed time, Buckie and Karl could be heard approaching the crag. Conversation for the past hour had been limited only to necessary details. Buckie was nervous, once more pushed well outside his comfort zone.

Drew paced around nervously as he heard Buckie and Karl approaching. They came into view, skirting along the bottom of the massive outcrop of gritstone that formed the crag. Drew stood statue still, focusing on Karl in an attempt to judge his mood. He recognised Karl as the watcher in the car park of the Lamb Inn. All three meeting participants were grim faced and for a few uncomfortable seconds, remained silent as if sizing each other up prior to battle. Karl broke the silence: "Ok, so where is it?"

Drew pointed towards the crag, then walked over to a point just a few metres from where they had met. Drew pointed once more, this time directly at the mossy crevice. Turning to face Buckie, Karl nodded his head sideways, gesturing towards the crack. Buckie understood the silent instruction and crouched like a midwife at the entrance to the fissure, rooting around in the opening with his extended arm. One by one, he delivered fifteen neatly wrapped packets of high potency cannabis from the crag. Each packet was the size of a bag of rice and contained a kilo of densely compressed dried cannabis buds. This cannabis was of the highly sought after variety that Karl and Otto had nurtured and jealously guarded over the past few years. Their "genetics". The street value of each compacted slab was around £3,500.

Karl unslung his rucksack from his shoulder and started loading the bags into it, he turned to Buckie and told him to disappear. Buckie was happy to comply and without any question or hesitation hastened back along the crag, to make his way down from the high moor.

Once Buckie was out of sight, Karl, elbow deep in the rucksack having just packed the last bag of cannabis away, turned to Drew and with a smile thanked him for handing over the cannabis. His smile slowly morphed into a scowl he then said "Sorry." Drew tucked in his chin in a puzzled expression, simultaneously taking a step backwards. "Sorry. About what?"

The answer came without further words. Without breaking eye contact with Drew, in a single movement Karl slowly rose to his feet and withdrew his hand from the rucksack. Drew could see the glint of metal in the faint light. Once again Drew found himself in a deadly predicament.

Drew's three mates had been focused on the proceedings, not wanting to miss any critical sign of impending trouble or danger. As Karl withdrew his loaded hand from the rucksack, Simon and Nick, alarmed at this escalation, automatically looked towards the spot where James was concealed. James was already standing straight, feet half a metre apart, shoulders aligned above his feet. Concentration and strain showed on his face.

Time slowed down for James. Crouching behind a group of boulders he had seen Karl withdraw the gun from the rucksack. In response, James had silently risen. Quickly loading an arrow, he automatically steadied his breathing as he applied the eighty pounds force needed to draw back the nock of the arrow to his cheek. A brisk wind was blowing from the north-east and James instinctively computed the adjustment he needed to make to his aim to compensate for its effect.

Maintaining his aim on Karl, James hesitated for a second. He optimistically hoped that Karl was simply intending to scare Drew, to deter him from any further interference in his business. James was dismayed to see Karl slowly extend his arm, raising the gun towards Drew's face.

As he had done hundreds of times in practice and competition, James Slowly exhaled to stabilise his aim. He then steadily uncurled the index and middle finger of his right hand, releasing the taut bowstring and loosing the heavy arrow towards its target.

Milliseconds after the swish of fletchings brushed against the bow, James's arrow thumped into Karl at a speed of sixty metres per second, breaking the silence and breaking bone.

Karl's right arm dropped, he reflex-fired a shot from his hand gun. The bullet blasted deep into the soft ground less than a metre from Drew's feet. At the same moment Karl's knees crumpled, dropping him face down into the soft peat. James had hit his target perfectly. The arrow had smashed into Karl's right shoulder blade, disarming him in an instant.

Karl let out an involuntary scream as he lifted his face from the mud, turning to one side. The scream was followed by rasping breaths as the pain from a cracked scapula hit him like a hammer blow.

The previous night, James had prepared two arrows for his role riding shot-gun for Drew. He had adapted two blunt point arrows, by adding tight bindings of heavy copper wire to the four inches immediately behind the tips. Blunt point arrows are designed to kill small game by the shock of the impact, rather than by penetration. The addition of the copper wire was intended to add weight and momentum to increase their impact on the bigger prey that James had in mind.

Traveling at less than a tenth of the speed of a bullet fired from a handgun, the heavy, blunt arrow hit Karl with enough force to instantly neutralise him, but as James had hoped, lacked the penetrating power to cause a fatal injury.

Ignoring Karl's groans and shouts of rage, James walked over to his prone form and yanked on the shaft of the arrow, drawing it sharply from pulped flesh. He concealed the arrow from Karl's line of sight. Karl let out a yell and rolled on his side to face James, he assumed that he had taken a bullet from a silenced gun.

James then swiftly stooped, snatched the gun away from Karl and smashed its barrel against the top of a rock. He then dropped it back from his gloved hand alongside Karl and said "This is your problem. You get rid of it."

Karl didn't appear to absorb James's words. He was struggling to breathe through the nauseating waves of pain that passed through his body, while attempting to gauge the extent of the damage he had sustained. Karl looked up to see Drew and three other guys with blackened faces looming over him.

James stood looking down into Karl's eyes and said: "You're not in much of a position to negotiate, so just listen. You have a simple choice to make. In a few moments, we are going to walk away from here. When we do, you will either be sinking into oblivion in one of the deep bogs up here or you will have about an hour of pain until Mountain Rescue reach you and trip you out with a shot or two of morphine. To avoid disappearing into the bog, you must agree to what I am about to say: We'll hide the drugs somewhere safe until you are in a position to collect them. Within the next ten weeks, you get in touch with us through Buckie, who will contact Drew to arrange the pickup. But next time you take the drugs and walk away. Then we call an end to this whole business. No shooting, no revenge…. What do you say?"

Karl responded in stinted gasps: "OK, I'll agree. I'll leave you guys alone. Just get me help. I'm in agony. I can hardly breathe."

James: "Where's your phone?"

Karl indicated that his phone was in his jacket pocket. James fished it out and said "OK, I'm going to dial 999 and hand the phone to you. When they answer, tell them you need Police, Mountain Rescue and that you have been injured on Bleaklow. They will ask for accurate location details, but just tell them you don't know. They have a system called SARLOC which can locate you from your phone signal, so just keep the call live until they arrive.

From Drew's previous questioning of Buckie, James was confident that following Otto's demise, Karl was now working alone. There was no risk that he could call an accomplice to try to intercept them on their way off the moors.

James picked up the rucksack which Karl had loaded up with the packages of drugs and rejoined Drew, Nick and Simon to commence their walk back to their vehicles.

Pointing to the gun, Karl shouted "Wait, what about this?"

James jogged back to Karl's side, picked up the gun with his gloved hand and hurled it into one of the many deep bogs which surround the crag. He then turned and ran to rejoin his friends for the walk off the moors.

Silence hung over the group for the first twenty minutes of their walk, until it was broken by Simon.

"Do you really believe he'll take the drugs and then that's the last we'll see of the bastard?"

Drew: "No, I don't. What did we expect him to say? *"Oh, you'd better throw me into the bog coz I'll be coming after you as soon as I'm fixed up."* He's not the sort to let sleeping dogs lie. In his business weakness means its game over."

James: "Yep. You're right, but we couldn't simply execute him up there. I know we've crossed some pretty shady boundaries lately, but we're not murderers."

Nick: "Of course we couldn't just kill him, but we'd better watch our backs from now on. Especially Drew. He only really knows Drew's face."

Simon, gesturing towards the bulging rucksack: "Another thing; what are we going to do with that lot?"

James: "Good question. It's our only collateral, the ace up our sleeve. I don't think Karl would do anything that would jeopardise his chances of getting it back. We need to hide it safely away again."

Apart from the odd spliff during their college and uni years, the drug scene was totally alien to the Wednesday Club members. They were all nervous about being in possession of such a large quantity of cannabis, so they hastily agreed that they needed to dispose of the drugs immediately. They decided to bury the drugs in a large featureless area of moorland, take accurate map coordinates and commit the location to memory.

They stopped to scrutinise maps for a suitable location. They needed somewhere remote, away from paths and features that might attract attention. James proposed a solution. Rather than having to commit a ten-figure numeric sequence of map coordinates to memory, they settle on a location which would be simple to remember and to relocate. They diverted onto Shining Clough Moss and using GPS located the precise spot that falls within the top loop of the letter "g" of the label on the Ordnance Survey map.

Using makeshift tools improvised from cut down plastic water bottles, they quickly dug a four-foot deep hole in the soft peat into which they crammed the laden rucksack. Ten minutes later the hole was backfilled and marked with two large and distinctive stones they found nearby.

While the Wednesday Club members had been preoccupied with hiding the cannabis once more, Karl had been fighting for his life high on Bleaklow. His injury wasn't life threatening in itself, however the pain combined with the sub-zero temperatures had caused his body to go into shock. By the time the first members of the Mountain Rescue team had reached him, he was grey and hypothermic. He was fortunate that he had dressed appropriately for what he knew would be a cold trek on the moors. His choice of clothing had provided valuable insulation buying him crucial survival minutes.

Karl was taken to hospital in Sheffield, where he spent four days recovering from the ordeal and having his wound assessed and treated. Medics and doctors were baffled by the nature of his injury, it looked like a gunshot wound, but Karl insisted that it had happened when he slipped and fell while descending from the top of the crag, landing awkwardly on a sharp rock.

CHAPTER 15

The Cave

Early May 2019

Over two months had gone by since the Wednesday Club members' violent misadventure on the high moors. They were still struggling through the emotional turmoil caused by the outcome of their own deeds. Despite Otto and Karl being ruthless and dangerous parasites on the skin of humanity, the four strived to rationalise and justify the events which culminated in the death of Otto and the serious wounding of Karl.

Eventually, James, Drew, Nick and Simon were all able to compartmentalise their traumatic experiences and pull back their lives to a semblance of normality. Each of the four guys dealt differently with the burden of having taken a life. James seemed the most resilient, he was the first to drag himself from the depths of the emotional abyss. He had the ability to apply black or white analysis to most problems and to move on without further self-questioning once he had reached a conclusion. Simon, Nick and Drew had taken longer to work their way through the process of self-justification.

Wednesday Club events had been sparse for a while. Their first outing since they left Karl on the moors to be found by the mountain rescue team, was intended to thoroughly exorcise any stubborn demons. They were still nervously awaiting contact from Karl. Only when the cannabis had been handed over and Karl had disappeared into the sunset, would they be able to fully relax and move on with their lives.

They returned to the scene of their misadventure; the Dark Peak.

They four guys were focused on getting back to the simple basis for the Wednesday Club's existence, that is participation in exciting, adventurous activities. They unanimously decided to draw a line under the Karma delivery idea, that had taken them into distinctively shady territory.

Simon had proposed their latest adventure. An attempt to discover the long-lost entrance to what could be a huge cave system.

For over a hundred years there had been rumours of the existence of an unexplored cave system on the Northern edge of Kinder Scout.

In 1862 an article in The Sheffield City News told the story of three adventurous teenagers, who had searched for and found the cave system. With only candles to light their way through the dark they became lost in its depths. They had been marking their way by scribing arrow marks on the rock walls of the cave, but on their excitement at discovering a vast chamber had strayed out of sight of their latest waymarker. Fortunately, after around six hours of searching the dark recesses of the chamber they found the lost arrow and made a rapid retreat, relieved to arrive back at the entrance, having almost exhausted their stock of candles. They had spent over eight hours below ground.

Published records state that around 1890, the entrance to the cave was sealed up by local shepherds who had been losing sheep, which had wandered into the entrance of the cave. Apparently while the opening of the cave was quite level, there were steep drop-offs into what was rumoured to be a bottomless chasm.

Nobody has set eyes on or foot in the cave since.

The four Wednesday Club members agreed unanimously that a search for this mythical, lost cave system would be a worthwhile adventure.

In preparation for the search, the team Google-searched, visited libraries and sought out local knowledge which might give them clues to where the cave entrance is located. A week of concerted effort turned up a varied selection of information including news articles, diary notes and even a copy of an ink drawing, which purported to show the cave entrance before it had been concealed by the concerned shepherds.

From the information they uncovered, they were very confident that the cave did exist, not just in mythology and the minds of wishful believers. Corroboration came in a wide variety of type and from numerous independent sources.

The fact that some of the information was contradictory added to their conviction. This wouldn't be the case if a single story or rumour had simply been retold and circulated, giving birth to a myth.

After a detailed and methodical analysis of the clues they had accumulated, they narrowed down their search area to a one hundred metres square patch of steeply sloping moorland, south of Snake Pass, high on the flank of Kinder Scout.

Armed with printed copies of the ink sketch the four Wednesday Club members once more ventured out onto the moors and hills of the Dark Peak. Their spirits were raised by the warm May day. The feel of the sun and the singing of skylarks was a welcome contrast to the conditions and the brutal events they had endured on their previous visit.

To give them a head start on the numerous tourists and hikers they expected would be visiting the area, they arrived on the moor at 5.00 a.m. just before the sun had started to appear over the horizon. The early start gave them sixteen hours of daylight in which to search for the cave entrance.

Their intention was to cover every square foot of the target area until they found the cave. They anticipated that this might necessitate quite a few return visits.

The four guys searched their chosen target area methodically, breaking it down into a grid of ten metre by ten metre squares. They then based their search on the assumption that the sketch they had acquired was reasonably accurate in its depiction of the cave entrance penetrating the hillside at a steep section of terrain.

Ignoring grid squares which contained only level ground or shallow gradients they focused their efforts on the squares containing sufficient vertical incline to accommodate the opening. Using this technique, by the time the sun was going down they had completed a preliminary scan of the whole target area and identified eight locations, which appeared to match their criteria. Recording GPS coordinates for each potential site, they trekked to the nearest pub in Hayfield for a beer and snack before heading off to their homes.

They returned the following day to carry out more detailed scrutiny of the eight promising sites they had identified. One by one they examined their slopes and paced around the areas to establish whether the surrounding contours and features of the terrain matched the details of the ink drawing. As the use of the moorland in the search zone hadn't changed over the past two-hundred years, they were confident that there would be no significant changes to the landscape.

Two of the locations were a possible match, with skyline and terrain roughly approximating to that shown by the sketch.

They split into two pairs, James and Simon investigating the lower level site, Drew and Nick focusing on the higher-level site. Using carbon fibre tent poles, they prodded and probed the steep sloping hillside, investigating any hollows or uncharacteristic sounds by crouching on hands and knees to dig with trowels.

James and Simon dug a whole warren of holes on their patch, to investigate the hollow knocks it consistently produced when struck with the metal ferrules on the ends of their poles.

James joked: "If anyone spots all these holes we can blame the rabbits."

One of the exploratory holes Simon dug exposed some rotting wood.

Simon: "This is strange. There are no trees up here but I can see some rotting tree branches in this hole. Wait a minute! Something that looks like hessian sacking too."

James: "That's promising. Maybe the shepherds used tree branches and sacks to block the entrance before backfilling it with peat."

Spurred on by the find, Simon and James dug frantically around the tree remnants and sack cloth. Digging deeper, they began to expose whole tree branches which were so well preserved they could even identify the type of tree as birch. The waterlogged acidic peat had helped to preserve the wood and the sacks by excluding oxygen. The very same natural chemistry was responsible for the preservation of the remains of the sacrificed ancient Briton known as Pete Marsh that was found in Lindow Moss in Cheshire.

Energised by the discovery, Simon jogged up to where Nick and Drew were digging: "Hey, you two, we think we've found something interesting down there. Come and have a look."

With the additional effort provided by Nick and Drew, they quickly revealed more birch branches and sacking.

James: "Assuming this is the cave entrance, let's try to keep any opening small, then we won't have much trouble covering it back up until we're ready to disclose it."

A further hour's probing and digging produced an opening, through which the four guys could peer. One by one, head torches set to high, they craned their necks into the hole. They were all excited by what they saw; a narrow slot through a vertical section of gritstone ran around six metres into the hillside. At the back of the cleft their torch beams hit a solid slab of rock which initially seemed to indicate the full extent of the cave. On further inspection however, they saw that the rock floor disappeared into blackness three metres or so from the rear of the cave. This really could be an entrance to the lost cave system.

They squeezed through the small opening they had created and taking care to place their feet on something more substantial than thin air, lined up single file to inspect their cramped surroundings. Light from their torches played on the damp and creviced walls, roof and floor of a cavern that hadn't seen the light of day for over a hundred years.

They made their way towards the back of the cleft, which opened out sufficiently to enable all four guys to stand and peer down into a gaping opening in the cave floor. Torch beams picked out a ledge around two and a half metres below. Beyond the ledge a yawning chasm opened out, swallowing up the light from their torches. Straining eyes eventually focused on faint light reflecting off some vague shapes in the depths. They estimated the bottom of the shaft to be around thirty to forty metres below.

Simon was mesmerised by the dark void. James noticed him staring into its depths, transfixed.

James: "Be warned Simon. Didn't Nietzsche say, "stare into the abyss for too long and the abyss will stare back at you". Or something along those lines?"

Nick: "Who's Nietzsche?"

Simon laughing: "Germany's answer to Confucius."

Drew: "This is no time for philosophy. Drew says its time to get the ropes out."

The guys eagerly shuffled back towards daylight to collect their rucksacks. At the front of the line, Nick stopped abruptly causing a conga pile-up.

Simon: "What's up Nick?"

Nick: "Simultaneously pointing his torch-beam and his finger towards the cave wall."

Craning necks to see around each other, all four explorers stared open-mouthed at the object of Nick's attention. Carved into the rock of the cave wall, illuminated by daylight streaming in through the newly created opening, was a chilling warning:

What man dares pass beyond this stone
Shall no more see the light of day
But in this abyss his breath will fade
This stone will mark his lonely grave

Drew: "Wow that makes the hair on the back of your neck stand up. I wonder who carved it."

Nick, laughing: "Maybe the shepherds, hoping their sheep can read."

As the guys rooted out the ropes and climbing gear from their rucksacks, the sun dazzled their eyes in sharp contrast with the darkness they had just left behind.

Being the most experienced in rock climbing and ropework, James and Drew each rigged up a rope for abseiling. They anchored two ropes to the rock at the entrance level, above the dark drop-off, inserting climbing devices known as wires and hexes into crevices, to which they attached karabiners. Their ropes were sixty metres long. If their guess at the depth of the chasm was reasonably accurate, they would be left with some margin for error, even allowing for five or six metres of rope needed for rigging up the system.

James and Drew took the precaution of tying stop-knots in the end of the ropes. The knots would ensure they wouldn't drop off the end of their ropes into oblivion if the chasm was deeper than they had estimated. They then put on their climbing harnesses, fed the ropes through their belay devices and readied themselves at the lip of the rock above the drop.

They had attached jumar rope ascending devices to gear loops on their harnesses. These were essential for the laborious climb back up the ropes.

When abseiling, no matter how many times you've done it, the first step over the edge is always daunting. James and Drew were no exception, however once they had made their first cautious move onto the vertical face of the chasm, their confidence grew and they trusted their lives to the rope and to their own skill. They dropped quickly, using their feet to push themselves away from the rock, they hopped around the ledge they had spied and then made a rapid descent into the darkness, competing with each other to be the first to land at the bottom. Peering down sideways, over their shoulders, they saw the cave floor rapidly approaching. They hit the bottom with a controlled bump. Voices echoing off the hard rock surfaces, they shouted up to Nick and Simon, who were stationed at the entrance level of the cave, to let them know they had safely completed their descent.

Nick shouted from above: "What's it like down there? Any spectacular stalactites or stalagmites?"

Drew responded laughing: "No chance mate. This is all gritstone. You only get stalactites and stalagmites in limestone caves. Did you not do geology at school?"

James and Drew remained attached to their climbing ropes, while they familiarised themselves with their surroundings. It was possible that they might be perched on a ledge, with further drop-offs nearby, so this was a sensible precaution. They discovered that they were stood in a roughly elliptical chamber approximately six metres across at its widest point and four metres at its narrowest. On touching down, their feet had become instantly cold and wet, they had landed knee-high in chilled, flowing water.

From the history they had learned of the cave, they had expected to land in a sheep's graveyard cluttered with bones, but it seemed likely that the water streaming through this level must have swept any traces of misadventurous sheep, into the cave system's lower levels.

Two openings led off through the walls of the chamber, both around a metre and a half high and one metre wide. Water flowed in through one and out through the other. From the sound of rushing water coming from the outflow tunnel, it was obvious that it dropped off steeply, hurling the water in torrents down into the depths of the earth. James edged slowly to the point where the water gushed out through the opening, making a mental note of what he saw for future exploration possibilities. As this passage led deeper into the hillside, he assumed that it was more likely to lead to other chambers and routes than the inflow channel.

After inspecting the chamber, they decided it was time to leave the damp, oppressive darkness, to rejoin their two mates. Caving is a very different sport to climbing and, more at home on the hills than inside them, both James and Drew had begun to feel claustrophobic. Using their jumar devices and slings, they ascended their ropes. This was difficult work compared to the ease with which they had descended. Gravity can be a bitch. After twenty minutes of energy sapping effort, they clambered back onto the ledge, below the cave entrance, pausing briefly before scrambling up the last short section to where Nick and Simon were waiting.

After James and Drew had informed Simon and Nick of their findings at the cave bottom, the four guys left the cave into the welcoming daylight. Excited by their rediscovery of the cave system and proud that their clever search methods had paid off, they debated what they should do next.

Simon: "We should cover it up to make it safe and notify the National Park authorities."

Drew: "I think we should get the local caving clubs involved, this is a big, historical find."

James had been uncharacteristically silent during the discussion, his mind clearly distracted.

James: "I think we should relocate Karl's drugs here and seal it up until we hear from him. Then once we've got rid of them, we can announce our discovery to the World."

Nick: "What? Why move the drugs from where they are? They're safely buried."

James: "Its been on my mind for a while. Yes, we've buried them safely, but Karl isn't going to disappear without his drugs and none of us wants to transport them to him, so its very likely that one day soon, we'll have to meet him again so he can collect them. I'm not happy about the prospect of meeting him on the open moors. There's no cover out there and we'll all be vulnerable if he turns up with weapons or back up. If he has to go into the cave to collect them, the situation will be far more controllable."

The three other Wednesday Club guys all agreed with James's suggestion. Simon and Nick headed off to Shining Clough Moss to recover the buried hoard of cannabis while James and Drew hastily covered the narrow entrance to the cave with the same materials they'd dragged from the ground to expose it. While the location of the cave entrance is remote, they didn't want to risk it being spotted by passing hikers.

Simon and Nick returned two hours later with the illegal load still safely contained within its rucksack, which had become blackened and damp from its temporary interment. Once again, they exposed the cave entrance and all four filed into the darkness. They lowered the drugs onto the ledge below the drop-off, where it was concealed in dark shadow. With the stash once more safely squirrelled away, they hastily covered the cave entrance. This time making every effort to ensure it blended as closely as possible with the surrounding hillside.

CHAPTER 16

Heads Up

Late May 2019

During his discussions with Buckie, Karl had gleaned enough background information about Drew to be able to pass himself off as a friend of his. Armed with this information, Karl wandered over to the visitor centre at the nature reserve where Drew volunteered his time. "Visitor centre" was a slightly ambitious title for the hut. It was home to a few information boards, a scattering of unmatching chairs and tables, collection boxes and a meagre selection of snacks and hot and cold drinks. Karl bought a coffee and a packet of biscuits and feigned interest in the display boards, which informed visitors of which species of birds they might be lucky enough to see from the hides scattered around the reserve.

Karl hung around in the centre until the opportunity arose to engage in conversation with the lone volunteer attendant, Geoff. He asked after Drew, inquiring whether he might be on the reserve today. Geoff was pleased to have someone to talk to, it had been a very quiet and dull day. Without much effort, Karl managed to obtain a few useful snippets of information about Drew.

On Drew's next shift at the nature reserve, he was signing in at the desk in the visitor centre, when Geoff mentioned his recent encounter. "Did your foreign friend manage to get in touch with you yet Drew?"

Alarmed, Drew stopped dead and turned to face Geoff: "What foreign friend?"

Geoff: "Big blond guy. Old friend of yours. Speaks good English but with a strong accent, German, or maybe Dutch."

Drew's skin prickled. Leaving Geoff gaping and bewildered at his quick exit, he dropped the pen, ran back to his car and sat in the driver's seat scratching his head. What did this mean? Karl had agreed to get in touch through Buckie when he was ready to collect his precious property.

Karl was clearly going to play this game by his own rules.

Drew spiralled into in a state of panic, believing that Karl was obviously on his trail. He called James from his car: "What do we do about this? Who knows what he's planning to do? We all know he's an evil bastard, capable of anything."

James: "Try not to panic mate. We're all behind you and we can handle this. We've got to face reality, he's obviously targeting you, so we need some way that you can alert us if the shit hits the fan."

Drew: "I always have my mobile on me."

James: "Yes but if Karl does get up to something, you can be sure the first thing he'll do is to take your phone from you. We need to think of something less obvious."

After a few moments' silent pause, James continued: "I've got an idea that should work. You know my uncle Frank has dementia? I got him a brilliant watch with an SOS button he can press to automatically alert me and my sister if he needs help. It also has an inbuilt GPS tracker that alerts us if he moves more than twenty metres from its Bluetooth base station. It then shows his location in real time on an app on our phones. How would you feel about wearing one just 'till this whole thing is resolved? I can set it to send an alarm signal to me, Simon and Nick."

Drew: "Sounds a bit big brotherish, but for a good reason. It's a good idea mate. It'll be reassuring to know I can get in touch in an emergency. Karl's obviously plotting something and as we've discovered, he's a nasty bastard."

James laughing: "It's quite a cool looking watch by the way."

The following day James visited the specialist shop from which he had bought his uncle's SOS tracker watch and bought a second one.

CHAPTER 17

Midnight Intruder

By combining information he had extracted from Buckie, with what he had gleaned from Geoff, Drew's chatty colleague at the nature reserve, Karl had managed to piece together a useful profile of Drew's circumstances and habits. He had traced Drew's address from his car registration and spent three weeks tracking his movements. He would use this knowledge to gain advantage in his plans to take back possession of his valued drugs and to take revenge both for the humiliation and for the physical injury he had suffered through the actions of the Wednesday Club.

Karl's approach to any conflict was based on the principle of getting to Know as much as possible about his adversaries.

While Karl was confident that Drew would stay home for the night following a shift at the nature reserve, he drove by Drew's house at midnight to make sure his car was still on the drive. He then parked in a quiet side road around half a mile away and set his alarm for 2.30 a.m.

Karl's alarm stirred him from a fitful doze in the chill of the night. Pushing himself up in his car seat, Karl wiped the condensation from the car windscreen and windows to allow him a clear view of the street. He winced at the pain that shot across his upper back and shoulder and paused to rub away the ache. The wound that James's arrow had inflicted on his shoulder blade had long since healed, but the jolt from damaged nerves served as a timely reminder of one reason for his nocturnal mission that night.

Karl extracted a small wooden box and a photograph from his car's glove compartment, slipped these into his coat pocket and then reached behind his seat, picking up a heavy, flat leather sheath. A smile played across his lips as he extracted a wooden handled machete from the sheath and inspected it. Taking care not to cut himself, he lightly ran his gloved finger along its razor-sharp edge. The honed blade reflected dull yellow light from the streetlamp across the road.

Karl had one last item to collect from his car before setting off on foot to pay Drew an uninvited visit. He reached below the passenger seat and pulled out a latex mask. The face of a pig. Not the face of a nursery rhyme pig, but a hideous, tusked and warty visage befitting any horror film. Karl had chosen this particular mask, not just to disguise himself from any prying CCTV system, but for shock value. He had learned that fear and terror are great allies in any confrontation or combat situation.

Karl stuffed the mask into his coat pocket, gripped the handle of the unsheathed machete in his gloved hand so that its blade was concealed along the length of his forearm and exited his car. Moving stealthily, he pulled up the hood of his coat, quietly closed and locked the driver's door and strode around to the footpath.

Karl ducked into a narrow alley close to his parked car, where he donned the pig mask. Keeping to the shadows where possible, he strode at a fast pace to the front gate of Drew's house. There he paused to check for any late-night on-lookers before cautiously opening the wrought iron gate, creating a narrow gap just wide enough to squeeze through.

Modern doors and locks are not the push-over most crime dramas would have you believe, whereby a quick jiggle and twist with a thin metal blade sees it conveniently open. Karl had to use his imagination in order to gain access into Drew's home.

Karl pulled the wooden box from his coat pocket. It was a clockwork, child's music box; the loudest one stocked by the gift store he had visited the previous week. He fully wound the music box mechanism and placed it on the footpath three yards down the street from Drews front gate. He opened the music box so that it played its slightly out-of-tune, metallic lullaby. He then slipped through the open gate, closing it behind him and in complete contrast to his stealthy approach to this point, banged loudly on the glass panel in Drew's front door. Karl then slipped around the side of the house, crouching low behind three wheelie bins.

Drew was startled awake by the noise and throwing on his dressing gown, ran downstairs to investigate. After glancing into each room, he opened the front door and peered out. At first glance nothing seemed out of order. Had he imagined the banging? Could it have been a car backfiring? He stood dead still on the front step listening for any other signs of disturbance. He heard metallic, tinkling music coming from the street. Puzzled by the sound, he sidled past his car and looked over the gate. He could see nothing, but the music was louder now. Curiosity killed the cat, it is also regularly responsible for dire consequences in humans. Drew followed the sound trail until he saw a small wooden box tucked in against the front wall of his garden. He bent down, picked it up, closed and opened the lid a few times and took it with him to inspect it by the external light next to his front door.

Drew, already on high-alert, sub-consciously looked down at the SOS tracker watch strapped to his wrist. The incident had spooked him, but what did it amount to? He couldn't very well press the panic button, metaphorically or literally, because he had been wakened by a noise and then found a child's toy in the street. Maybe the bang had been made by someone throwing the music box out of a passing car.

Feeling chilled by the night and by the awakening, he locked the front door behind him, went into his kitchen and examined the music box while waiting for the kettle to boil. He took a comforting cup of tea upstairs and climbed back into bed to read for a while. Reading made him drowsy and after half an hour he was sleeping again.

Karl's ruse had worked. While Drew had been crouching to examine the music box, he had sneaked from his hiding place behind the bins, slipped into Drews house and concealed himself behind a bed in the smallest of Drew's three bedrooms. He had been ready for action, anticipating that Drew might discover him hiding, but he much preferred to wait until Drew was sleeping again before moving to the next stage of his plan. The element of surprise is an effective weapon.

Disturbed from deep REM sleep, Drew felt a warm, sticky wetness on the left side of his face. Half wakened, thinking the room must be too hot and that he had been sweating, he wiped his cheek with the back of his hand. The dense stickiness and the unmistakable metallic aroma of blood dragged him from the depths of his dreams.

As Drew sat up, he was hit by a searing pain on his scalp and he felt the warm trickle of blood tracking down his cheek onto his neck.

His heart pounding in his chest and sweat beginning to bead on his brow, Drew's eyes adjusted to the dim half-light of his bedroom. A looming shadow came into focus at the foot of his bed. This was some bad dream. As his vision sharpened, the shadow slowly took the form of a pig. A pig standing well over six feet tall. Horror-struck, Drew bolted upright and reached for the bedside lamp. Lit by the light from the lamp, Drew saw that the pig was holding a machete in its human right hand.

The pig spoke from behind its grotesque mask: "It's been a while Drew."

On hearing the heavy Dutch accent, Drew immediately realised what this hellish intruder was. He also knew the purpose of its visit and instantly regretted hot having pressed the panic button when he had been disturbed earlier that night.

Karl moved closer to Drew, brandishing the machete blade near his face. "Where's my property?"

Drew: "What the hell have you done to me?"

Karl: "Its just a nick. I needed to wake you up and I also need you to know how sharp my blade is. Now answer me. Where is my property?"

Drew: "Safely stored, like we promised. I can get it and bring it to you later today. Then we're quits. Right?"

Karl: "You're staying with me 'till I get what's mine. Get up and get dressed. You're going to get the stuff for me right now. Oh and just to make sure you cooperate I have a something for you."

Karl then produced a photo from his pocket, handing it to Drew. On viewing it Drew gasped and looked up into Karl's pig eyes: "What the hell is this?"

Karl: "Don't you recognise your own son? I drove all the way to Cardiff to take this. I know exactly where Scott lives. I hear he is a good swimmer, but I bet he couldn't swim across Cardiff Bay with chains around his ankles."

Drew, terrified that Scott might be in danger: "Okay, okay, I'm not going to mess anything up. Like we promised, the drugs are safely hidden away ready for you. I'll take you there now."

Karl: "Yes you're fucking right you'll take me there now. Hurry up and get some clothes on and give me your phone. This time you won't have the chance to arrange for your mates to rescue you."

Drew picked up his mobile phone from the bedside table and handed it to Karl. He decided not to push the SOS button on his watch. Even if he was certain he could do it unnoticed by Karl, Drew didn't want to risk provoking an attack from this violent psychopath. Nor did he want to risk putting Scott in harms way. Did Karl have associates he could call on to hurt Scott?

Shaken and fearful, Drew cleaned the blood from his head and face in the bathroom, then he dressed in warm clothes and walking boots for the impromptu trek into the hills.

Karl watched Drew closely to ensure he maintained the advantage and control his nightmarish intrusion into Drew's life had gained him. The tip of the machete was never more than an arm's length from Drew, although Karl could sense that this really wasn't necessary. The photo of Drew's son and the clear threat to Scott's life would ensure Drew's total compliance.

Once dressed, Drew collected a couple of head torches and two bottles of water. He silently followed Karl's prompts and instructions. They climbed into Karl's car. Karl drove, while Drew obediently provided directions to their destination in the Dark Peak. Silence filled the car until they reached their destination on the outskirts of Hayfield, where they parked along a quiet lane, close to the start of a footpath that leads onto Kinder Scout.

Karl dragged a large rucksack from the back seat and instructed Drew to get out of the car and put it on. They walked to the edge of the moors, clambered over a stile and started up one of the rough stony paths. The moonless night was pitch black. A blanket of cloud shut out light from the stars, so the head torches were essential in finding their way. Drew put to use the night navigation skills he had developed over years of hill walking.

CHAPTER 18

Red Alert

Not wanting to run the risk of violent repercussions from their intervention, Drew had taken the decision not to use the SOS function of his newly acquired tracker watch. In the panic and confusion of the night's events he had forgotten the Wander Alert function.

The wander alert simultaneously buzzed on James's, Simon's and Nick's phones. James and Simon woke instantly, Nick slept on, undisturbed. Concerned that Drew was unexpectedly outside the wander zone perimeter, James and Simon both reacted in the same way, they logged onto the tracker watch app to check Drew's location. Transfixed by the blue dot wandering slowly across their phone screens, they watched as Drew drove out of town, heading in the direction of Hayfield. This could only mean one thing; Karl was pulling the strings.

James called Simon and Nick, who awoke from deep sleep at the sound of his ring tone. During hasty phone calls the three Wednesday Club mates agreed that they should head up into the Dark Peak to try to intercept Drew. As the alert had come from the passive wander-alert function of Drew's watch and not the SOS function they had to assume that Drew had been taken by surprise, possibly forcibly.

James's wife Ann was wakened by the phone call. She was accustomed to his unconventional lifestyle and to his regular nocturnal comings and goings. All part of being married to one of life's adventurers, but there was something in the tone of James's voice that troubled her as he wandered room to room phone pressed to his ear, with Freddie the dog circling him curiously.

Ann: "What's going on James?"

James gestured for Ann to hush, so he could concentrate on his phone conversation.

When the call had finished, James hurriedly put on some clothes, causing Ann more anxiety.

"Why do you have to go out so urgently James? What's this about?"

James, thinking of an excuse that wouldn't alarm Ann: "It's the cave, Drew couldn't sleep and had a wander up there. He thinks somebody else has also discovered it. Perhaps we were seen there. We don't want someone else to beat us to it, so were rushing up there to do some more exploring."

Simon also had similar awkward questioning from his wife Deb to fend off. He wasn't as skilled as James in spontaneously spinning convincing explanations. As he left their house in a rush to join the others, he left Deb feeling ill at ease. What was so urgent it couldn't wait until morning?

While Deb liked James, she couldn't help feeling that sometimes he could be reckless and shady in his activities. She was becoming uncomfortable with Simon's Wednesday Club activities.

James threw on some clothes, picked up his head torch and rucksack and drove to Nick's and Simon's homes to pick them up. Once they were all together in James's Land Rover, early-hours drowsiness now driven off by the flow of adrenaline, they had to quickly decide on a plan of action.

It was clear from the tracker that Drew was heading towards Hayfield. This indicated conclusively that he was heading to the cave. Drew had a half-hour start on them, but they hoped to reduce the lead by using a different route.

James, Nick and Simon drove through Glossop onto Snake Pass. During the day this would be the slower option due to traffic congestion which plagues that spectacular road, but at this early hour they knew it was unlikely that they would encounter any other vehicles. While their drive to Snake Pass would add around fifteen minutes to the road journey, their trek on foot to the cave would be around three kilometres shorter than the route from Hayfield. They calculated that the overall time saving would be around twenty minutes, so they expected to arrive at the cave around ten minutes later than Drew.

To avoid their arrival triggering a violent reaction from Karl and any accomplice that might be along for the collection, James, Nick and Simon decided that they should make a stealthy approach to the cave and use the element of surprise to their advantage in any conflict that might arise.

Keeping an eye on the map of the tracker watch app, James, Nick and Simon hurried across the dark moorland terrain. In such black conditions a normal head torch beam can be seen many miles away, so to avoid alerting Karl to their pursuit they switched their head torches to red light mode and ensured that the faint beams were directed downwards at all times.

CHAPTER 19

Staring into The Abyss

Karl had always prided himself in maintaining a high level of fitness, so he was shocked by how tiring he found the uphill trek. On arriving at the point where Drew indicated they should stop, he doubled over panting to catch his breath. It crossed Drew's mind that this might be the only opportunity he would have to take Karl by surprise and to overpower him, however, he stuck to his original plan of compliance in the hope that once Karl had what he wanted, he would disappear from their lives for good. He could also sense that Karl's guard had not dropped. Despite his breathlessness, he maintained his vigilant watch over Drew, his hand firmly gripping the machete in readiness.

Drew told Karl that he needed to dig out the entrance to where the drugs were hidden. He had not gone into detail about the extent of the cave.

After fifteen minutes spent clearing away the turf, heather and ancient birch branches that the Wednesday Club guys had covered the hole with, a small opening into the hillside was visible.

Karl nodded towards the cave entrance, gesturing with his machete that Drew should go inside. Karl followed closely behind Drew. He was staggered by what he saw. This was clearly much more than a hole in the hillside. He looked around, studying his surroundings in the light from his head torch.

Drew risked a smile: "Amazing isn't it?"

Karl responded: "Not what I expected. Where is my property?"

Drew, pointed at the two coiled ropes, one of which was still anchored to the rear of the cave entrance: "I'll get it for you. It'll take a while as I have some climbing to do."

At this point, Karl still needed Drew if he was to accomplish his task, so Drew decided that it was the right time to raise the subject that he had been anxious to broach.

"It's understandable that you're pissed off with us, but once I recover your property for you, can I assume that you will stick by the agreement we made when we saved your life out on the moors? Can we call it quits and all get on with our lives?"

Karl, sneered: "You are not in a position to negotiate. You only saved my life because you and your friends endangered it in the first place. Your friend shot me in the back. What's more, I don't believe Buckie's story that my business was wrecked because some Manchester drug pushers happened to stumble across it. I think you and your friends have more to answer for than just my injured back."

Karl's response scared Drew. He thought back to the time on the moor when, had it not been for James's arrow, Karl would have coldly executed him on the spot. He feared for his own life, but more than that, he feared for his son. Scott was an innocent party in all this, but he felt that Karl wouldn't hesitate to take his revenge on him. In that moment, he decided that only one of them would be returning from the cave. The chilling carving inside the entrance would prove to be prophetic for either himself or Karl.

To abseil down the short drop without a climbing harness and friction devices would be an easy matter for Drew, however he decided to tie loops in the anchored rope to enable him to climb back up from the ledge where the drug stash was hidden. He realised that this was probably optimistic on his part, as it was likely that Karl intended to leave him lying at the bottom of the chasm once he had what he came for.

Drew explained his plan to Karl; he would clamber down to the ledge where the drug laden rucksack was concealed and then climb back to hand it over to Karl.

Karl, ever suspicious, wondered if Drew might try to descend further into the cave in order to escape. Might Drew be aware of exit routes which couldn't be seen from the upper level? He told Drew that he would watch his every move and if he wasn't happy about something, hell would be unleashed on Scott. Karl had quickly homed in on Drew's weakness, any mention of Scott brought on obvious signs of anguish.

Drew slowly and painstakingly tied eight loops in the rope, buying himself time to plan his next move or to spot a momentary opportunity to catch Karl off guard.

James, Nick and Simon had arrived at the entrance a few minutes after Drew had led Karl inside. Seeing that the entrance had been uncovered once more, they realised that Drew and Karl were in the cave. Keeping out of sight, torches switched off, they listened at the narrow opening. Hearing the discussion between Drew and Karl they decided to wait, hidden just outside the entrance to listen for any signs that Drew needed help after the handover had been completed. They could then take Karl by surprise and overpower him if necessary.

Illuminated by the beams from both head torches, Drew slowly lowered himself onto the narrow ledge, below the upper level from which Karl now peered down. On arriving at the ledge, Drew hauled the dirty rucksack containing Karl's precious cargo from the shadows and placed it over his shoulders. Using the loops in the rope as handholds and smearing his feet against the vertical rockface he climbed back to the upper level where Karl eagerly snatched the rucksack from him.

Karl placed the rucksack on the floor and impatiently opened the lid to check its contents. Realising that for first time that night, Karl had been distracted from his hawk-like vigilance, Drew decided that this would be his best, and maybe only, chance to make his move. He gripped the rope with both hands, wrists supported by rope loops and swung as forcefully as he could towards Karl.

The collision swept Karl off his feet and sent the rucksack tumbling over the edge, spewing packages of drugs as it bounced off the ledge below into the black abyss. In his peripheral vision, Karl had noticed Drew's rapid movement and anticipating the impact dropped his machete and flung his arms around Drew's neck at the moment of impact. The pair swung out over the chasm like a human pendulum. Drew had gripped the rope just above the level of the cave floor which, along with the stretch of the dynamic climbing rope, resulted in the two combatants slamming into the rock face below the drop-off from the cave's upper level. Karl took the brunt of the impact, hitting the unforgiving gritstone side on in a rib crunching collision, cushioning Drew from the worst of the impact.

Winded and wounded, Karl lost his grip on Drew and dropped from the tangle, his clothes and skin tearing against the rough surface of the rock as he plummeted downwards. He landed on the narrow ledge from where Drew had retrieved his drugs. Teetering close to the edge, Karl managed to swing his weight away from the massive drop. He was now shaken and afraid. He had given Drew good reason for wanting him dead and Drew now had the upper hand. His son had been threatened and this made Drew a dangerous adversary. Karl was angry at himself for underestimating Drew.

Karl grabbed at the rope which hung over the ledge, the end dangling over thirty metres below. Drew had anticipated his move and yanked at the rope in an attempt to retrieve it before Karl could use it to climb back to his level. The section of rope with the tied loops was now on the upper level, out of Karl's reach, but Karl managed to grab hold of the lower section of rope. Drew had the advantage; not only did he literally have the high-ground, but he had also managed to coil the rope around his hands enabling him to secure a strong grip on it. Ten millimetre diameter climbing rope is not easy to hold onto. Each time Karl gripped the rope, Drew yanked it firmly using the coils he had made, pulling it through Karl's grip, burning his skin. Hands bloodied by the futile effort, Karl gave up trying to grab the rope and leaned his back against the vertical rock face, gasping to fill his lungs with the oxygen desperately demanded by his body.

Drew managed to fully retract the rope and flung it towards the back wall of the cave, where it landed in an untidy heap.

On hearing the fracas, James, Nick and Simon rushed into the cave, fearing that their friend had been injured or worse. They were relieved to see Drew standing, panting, looking over the edge towards Karl.

Apart from rope burns to his wrists and scratch marks on his neck from Karl's frantic effort to hang on to him, Drew was physically unscathed. His mental state however was another matter. He was bordering on hysterical, repeatedly ranting "I'm going to kill that bastard. He's threatened to kill Scott!"

Nick and Simon tried to calm Drew down, while James kept an eye on Karl who was shouting for them to help him climb up off the ledge.

James shouted down to Karl: "You're in a shit state down there Karl. We've agreed once before that you'd call an end to hostilities. If we're going to help you, we need your categorical assurance that you'll comply with that. Drew says that you're threatening his son, so where does that leave us?"

Karl: "If you help me out of here. I'll stick to our agreement. I'll collect my property and piss off away from here, leaving you guys in peace."

Drew shouted at James: "Bullshit he will. He's already tried to kill me once and he's threatened Scott."

James: "Hear that Karl? Why should we trust you?"

Karl: "You can take my word, I swear on my child's life."

James told Karl that he would rig a rope and drop it down to him to enable him to join them at the upper level of the cave. Then James will abseil down to the bottom of the cave to retrieve the drugs, hand them to Karl and they will then part ways; permanently.

Looking up from his precarious position, Karl nodded his head in agreement.

Nick and Simon, hoping to finally draw a line under this whole debacle, immediately agreed with James's deal. They both moved to the edge of the drop where they tried to get an insight into Karl's mood by looking down into his eyes. Drew however took a step to the side, tight lipped and trembling he shook his head slowly.

James: "Sorry Drew, you're outvoted mate. We're all with you, but we need to finish this and get on with our lives."

James spent the next ten minutes re-rigging the knotted rope using the anchor system they had set up on their first visit. Apart from the clinking of climbing gear and the noise of James's breathing as he prepared the rope for Karl, the cave had fallen into eerie silence.

James carried the coiled rope over to the lip of the drop-off above Karl and threw the rope into the void, beyond Karl and the ledge. The rope's end disappeared into the darkness behind Karl, its rapid uncoiling caused it to whip to and fro until it stabilised under its own weight.

Relieved, Karl immediately grasped the nearest loop and then clumsily clambered up the rock wall. His feet scrabbled to gain purchase on the gritstone as he leaned his weight back using his arms to support himself. Karl teetered awkwardly, body angled out over the drop as his first foot reached the lip of the upper level.

In an unexpected burst of action, Drew leapt in front of James, pushing him backwards, grabbed the machete from the floor and swung it at the rope, severing it with a single swipe. The force of the blow tore the machete from Drew's hand and it bounced off the cave floor into the void below. A metallic clang rang out as it hit the bottom.

On realising what Drew's intentions were Nick shouted "No!" but it had been too late.

A look of horror swept across Karl's face and he desperately grabbed at thin air, but he managed to grasp more than just the air. One of his open hands hit Simon's ankle and instantly reflexed into a firm grip. Every ounce of Karl's strength poured into this last chance to save himself.

The force of Karl's swiping blow swept Simon's foot from beneath him, collapsing his legs. Simon's head whipped back hitting the rock. Momentarily stunned, he lost his balance and his ankle still firmly in Karl's grip, he was dragged over the edge by the momentum of Karl's fall.

Entangled, Karl and Simon toppled off the edge of the cave's upper level, bounced in tandem off the ledge below and disappeared into the chasm. Their desperate shouts were quickly followed by a sickening thud and splash as they hit the bottom of the shaft.

The whole horrific incident had lasted a mere couple of seconds but the surreal scene replayed in slow motion over and over in James' Nick's and Drew's minds. They would forever question themselves on their inability to act swiftly enough to save Simon.

Stunned into silence, James, Drew and Nick stood gawping into the black void down which their friend had plummeted. Their optimistic shouts were met by complete silence. Their dazed minds struggled to absorb the horror of what had just happened.

CHAPTER 20

Simon's Journey

As Simon toppled into the abyss in a commotion of tangled limbs and stomach-churning acceleration, images of Deb and his two sons flashed through his mind. A sense of total loss numbed his mind for the brief instant he was airborne. He had no time to register fear, but his mouth let out an involuntary, reflex shout of terror.

Then came the impact, a massive but surprisingly painless jolt. "Incredible" he thought. How could I have survived such a drop? Was my fall broken by Karl's body? Did the stream save me?"

Simon stood up. Looking around he could see the lower level of the cave in surprisingly clear detail. He looked up to see his three friends peering down, their anguished shouts echoing from the hard rock walls of the void through which he had just plummeted.

Simon called up to them. "I'm okay!"

No response came from above. He could hear his friends in their frenzied panic, trying to absorb the enormity of the incident and debating what action they must take.

Simon looked down at Karl's unmoving body and was instantly thrown into a state of confusion and alarm. Lying next to Karl was another broken body. "That looks like me! It is me. This doesn't make sense." Then the realisation hit Simon in a Tsunami of emotion. He hadn't survived the impact. That is, his physical body hadn't survived.

Simon felt a sickening panic rising through him, but this was a fleeting feeling, quickly replaced by a feeling of great calmness which seemed to come from an unseen but insistently pervading presence. He looked up towards his friends again and saw a fourth face looking down. Despite the dark and the distance, he recognised the face of his old friend Pete, who had died in a car accident three years ago. He instinctively knew that Pete was there to help him. As Simon continued to stare upwards, he saw the roof of the cave open-up to the night sky. A bright light shone through the opening, gradually increasing in intensity until everything and everyone was obliterated from view; apart from Pete who had become more distinct.

Simon sensed a surge of energy pulling him towards the light, however the feeling of panic had returned. Restrained by worries about what he was about to leave behind he remained anchored to the cave bottom. How would Deb and the boys manage without him? He would never see his grandchildren. What would happen to his business? Shit! no more adventuring with his close friends.

Feeling that he was being beckoned by Pete, an overwhelming sensation of peace pushed aside these earthly worries and Simon knew that he was about to embark on his biggest adventure yet. With these positive thoughts, he was freed from gravity's earthly grip and he allowed himself to be drawn up in a warm vortex of light, accepting Pete's guidance, as he embarked on his onward journey. As Simon rose past his Wednesday Club friends, he called to them, but they were absorbed with their own frenzied efforts. He knew that they hadn't heard his final goodbye.

Drew shuddered, a startled look in his eyes. He stood alert and still, only his eyes moving.

Nick: "What's up Drew?"

Drew: "Did you feel that?"

James: "Feel what?"

Drew: "A cold blast of air just came up from the cave. I felt it go right through me, chilled me to my bones."

CHAPTER 21

The Loss of a Friend

James snapped himself out of shock induced paralysis. He attached the remaining, intact rope to the anchor and positioned it around his body in readiness for a classic abseil. The friction required to control his rate of descent would be provided solely by the contact between his body and the rope. This was much more dangerous than using a climbing harness and friction device, but other than the ropes, they had no climbing gear with them.

James stepped off the edge, leaning back so that he could walk backwards down the vertical rockface. The first short hop down to the ledge below was easy. He then continued with the main part of the descent. After dropping around ten metres he lost his footing, his kneecap crunched into the harsh gritstone and his upper body swung uncontrollably into the rock wall. He twisted to take the impact on his shoulder and hip, simultaneously jolting his head as his head torch clashed against the rock. He bounced off the rock face spinning in mid-air for a few seconds until he was able to stabilise himself sufficiently to place his feet back against the vertical face. It had taken enormous self-control to resist the instinctive urge to use his hands to fend off the impact. Had he done so, he would have lost control of the rope and dropped like a stone to the bottom.

Before continuing his descent, James tightened his grip on the rope and held his position for a few seconds, to recover his breath and his composure. He was panting with exertion. The effort and the intimidating exposure caused stinging beads of sweat to drip into his eyes from his forehead.

James finally splashed down, landing awkwardly on the cave floor. Karl's head torch was still emitting light despite the fall. James gasped when he saw that his friend Simon was lying face down in the shallow, underground stream, limbs twisted into unnatural positions. Karl lay a short distance from Simon, the effects of the bone-crushing fall on him were all too obvious.

James gently lifted Simons head out of the water. Horrified at what he saw, James's eyes widened and he slowly lowered Simon's head back into the stream. The impact had inflicted a massive injury to Simon's skull. This vision would haunt James for many years.

James groaned in anguish and spontaneously vomited into the stream. In the violently spiralling events of the last few minutes he had lost one of his closest friends and he, Nick and Drew had been thrown neck-deep into a desperate predicament.

James briefly inspected Karl's broken body. He noticed the grip of a handgun protruding from below his hip, its barrel still tucked inside the waist of his jeans.

It was clear beyond any doubt that both Simon and Karl were dead. The severed rope, rucksack and packages of drugs were scattered around their two bodies.

James faced an arduous ascent back to the upper level of the cave. He needed to calm himself for the climb, but before he faced that task, he had work to do. Despite being in a state of distress, James forced himself to think through their position and to take decisive action to protect himself and the other two surviving Wednesday Club members.

James searched around the cave floor for the machete. He spotted it under the tumbling flow of water that swept through the cave and picked it up by the blade, stretching his sleeve over his hand to avoid depositing finger prints on it. He wiped it clean with his other sleeve and then momentarily wrapped Karl's dead hand around the handle. He then placed it on a dry section of rock, away from the stream.

James then tied himself onto the end of the rope and shouted up to Drew and Nick. He relayed the shattering news of Simon's death.

After a brief pause, he then asked Drew to prepare the rope for his ascent.

Due to the urgency of their late-night escapade, they hadn't thought to bring any climbing equipment with them. Without any friction device or cord which could be used to tie prusik knots, James wasn't able to climb up the rope. He had no alternative other than to climb the sheer rockface up to the cave entrance level, protected from falling by Drew's ropework skills.

Drew tied an Italian hitch in the karabiner of the anchor they had left in place. Using this climbers' slipping, friction knot, he belayed James as he made the hazardous ascent, ready to arrest any fall that James might take.

Keeping the rope taut, Drew hauled in the slack in time with James's slow progress up the rock, providing what they usually jokingly referred to as "a bit of anti-gravity assistance". The sharp gritstone cut into James, bloodying his fingers and scraping through his jeans to scuff skin from his knees and shins.

While James was an experienced rock climber, the vertical climb was a lung-burning struggle. Ledges and holds for hands and feet were sparse. On reaching the narrow ledge just below the entrance level of the cave, panting heavily, he paused to recover his breath before hauling himself over the lip to join his two friends. Nick helped him over this last hurdle while Drew maintained tension on the rope until James was safely away from the edge.

On James's arrival, Drew broke down sobbing and cursing himself for his action. His eagerness to destroy Karl had led to the death of his friend. The three remaining Wednesday Club members propped each other up in an emotional embrace. The loss of Simon was devastating to all of them.

James: "Don't blame yourself Drew. I found a gun with Karl's body. He would have killed us all. The three of us are lucky to be alive. When you untied the rope you'd cut with the machete, what did you notice about the way I'd tied it on to the Karabiner?"

Drew: "You'd tied a quick-release knot into the anchor. Why?"

James: "I'd made the same decision as you Drew. Karl had to die, otherwise we and our families would have been in real danger. I was going to wait until he was perched on the edge and then release the rope. You beat me to it; I was planning to kill Karl. If we had let Karl live then Simon would probably be dead now anyway, shot by Karl along with the rest of us. You took a calculated risk to protect us all."

Drew grasped at this opportunity to lighten his conscience: "Do you really believe that? I need to believe it."

James: "Yes its true…. I don't want to seem disrespectful to Simon. We've got the rest of our lives to grieve his loss, but we now need to decide how we protect ourselves."

Nick: "Protect ourselves? From what?"

James: "From being accused of murder and involvement in this whole drugs thing. We need to fabricate a plausible cover story for the situation we're in."

The three Wednesday Club members sat in the shadow of the cave, having temporarily put aside their pain and grief in order to focus their minds on the urgent task in hand. Within an hour they had agreed on a plan. Their story would be based on the truth, with a few imaginative twists to ensure that they would not be implicated in any crime.

They called the police and waited inside the cave for their arrival.

CHAPTER 22

The Wriggle

The police arrived on the scene around an hour after the call, accompanied by the local Mountain Rescue Team, which had been called out to guide the police to the location and to assist with any manoeuvring on dangerous terrain that might be required.

Out of necessity, James, Nick and Drew had had to refocus their traumatised minds away from the tragic loss of Simon into self-preservation mode. They concocted and rehearsed what they hoped was a plausible story, which would explain that night's events in the cave. It went like this:

James, Simon, Nick and Drew had become intrigued by the mythical "lost cave" and had spent a few weeks searching for it. They finally discovered it the day before the tragic incident and made a brief exploration of the upper level. The next night, they visited the cave again to make a more thorough exploration and on arriving, they discovered that someone else had very recently been in the cave, probably another hiker they thought, having been attracted by their activity. This bothered them as they were keen to be the first team to explore the cave's depths in over a hundred years. Simon had been lowering himself onto the ledge on which they had just spotted a rucksack, when they were attacked by an unknown man who had rushed into the cave. He slashed Simon's rope with a machete, causing Simon to tumble off the edge. As Simon was falling, he managed to grab the attacker and dragged him off the edge with him. On abseiling down to the cave floor, James had found Simon and the unknown man dead and they had alerted the police.

James, Nick and Drew diligently adhered to their story at each of the follow up police interviews they were subjected to. Any gaps in their observations were explained by the fact that apart from the light from head torch beams, the whole incident had happened in darkness, not to mention the confusion and panic caused by the attacker.

The police quickly concluded that Karl's presence in the area must be linked to the discovery of Otto's and Sonja's bodies. They decided to investigate this new incident alongside the ongoing, unsolved case that had hit the headlines as "The Bodies in The Pond".

During five weeks of intense investigation, the police detective team assigned to the case conjectured a chain of events that would explain the demise of four people. Their theory, mortared together by presumed motives and methods, conveniently wrapped up the murders of three foreign nationals and a local hiker.

The concluding police report surmised that Sonja had been a drug mule, used by Otto and Karl to bring cannabis into the UK from The Netherlands. Because of a dispute, she had been killed and her body dumped in the woodland pond. Later Karl and Otto had fallen out over some disagreement concerning their drug business, resulting in Karl shooting Otto and concealing his body alongside Sonja's corpse. Karl must have discovered the cave when searching the remote section of moorland for a suitable hiding place for drugs and hidden his stockpile there. By chance Karl returned on the night the four hikers had entered the cave, perhaps to remove some of the cannabis to sell and finding intruders there, assumed they were stealing his drugs. He then carried out the violent attack that resulted in his own death and that of one of the hikers.

The police congratulated themselves on achieving such a rapid resolution and no further action or investigation was deemed necessary, other than to inform Sonja's Serbian parents about her tragic death.

James, Nick and Drew were relieved to have been quickly identified as innocent victims, who had simply stumbled into the wrong place at the wrong time.

CHAPTER 23

The Funeral

The day of Simon's funeral was an emotional roller coaster for James, Nick and Drew. They were there to grieve, but also to celebrate the life of their lost friend and to acknowledge that his time here had been cut short. Far shorter than anyone could have expected. Carrying their burden of untold secrets, they were weighed down by a mixture of guilt and grief as they tried to provide support and comfort to the family Simon had left behind.

Simon's widow Deb had mixed feeling towards Simon's three Wednesday Club friends. They had known each other for many years and she appreciated that they had brought a great deal of fun and comradery to Simon's life, but she couldn't help feeling that had it not been for their involvement in his life, she would still have her husband in hers.

Simon hadn't been religious, in fact he had referred to himself not as an atheist, but as anti-religious. He felt that religion was by far the biggest cause of conflict, division and cruelty in the World, invented by the greedy few to control the minds of the masses.

Out of respect for Simon's beliefs, the funeral was a simple and quite brief affair held at the crematorium, without any input from religious officialdom.

Despite Simon's anti-religion stance, he didn't believe that death was the end. His own personal experiences had led him to believe that life was a temporary staging post; a learning experience. Simon's own model of understanding for the afterlife encompassed his own experiences, which included past-life memories he had experienced as a child and also unquestionable evidence of contact with his deceased parents through a renowned medium. Simon had always seen death as an inevitable adventure, not to be feared.

Out of respect for Simon's beliefs, Deb chose poignantly appropriate music for his funeral service. Not the usual, traditional dirges and hymns, but more modern pieces that reflected his beliefs; Don't Fear The Reaper by Blue Oyster Cult and It's All Been Done, by the Bare Naked Ladies.

James was one of three friends and family members who Deb had asked to prepare and read a tribute to Simon. He stood upright at the lectern to the side of Simon's coffin and delivered his eulogy with an appropriate mixture of solemnity and humour, occasionally glancing down at his notes. Partway through his reading, he noticed the door at the back of the chapel open partially as half a face peered through. The door then fully opened and in walked Buckie. Stooping, in an attempt to remain inconspicuous, he searched out a seat as close to the rear of the room as possible and quietly sat down, ignoring curious sideways glances from mourners.

On seeing Buckie's entrance, James couldn't prevent an involuntary frown appearing across his brow. Already holding back tears and struggling to maintain a strong, unquivering voice, he stumbled over a sentence. Coughing to help himself regain his composure, he managed to continue to the end of the tribute without further slip-ups. Nick and Drew picked up on James's body language and glanced backwards, they too frowned in puzzlement on seeing Buckie sat at the rear of the room, with a suitably mournful look on his face.

On conclusion of the service, the mourners filed out, some hanging back in the chapel garden to chat with Simon's family and to reminisce among themselves. James and his wife Ann, Nick and Drew stood together looking at the many wreaths and bouquets of flowers that had been lined up near to the exit. Simon's wife Deb came over to join them and after the consolatory greetings, she tersely broached an inquiring and awkward line of discussion.

"I just can't come to terms with Simon's death. I've read all the official reports on the accident and I've spoken at length to the police, but I can't help feeling that there's something more to what happened that night. It just seems such a tragic coincidence that at the very minute you all set out to explore the cave, this murderous thug turns up and flies into a violent rage. Simon seemed troubled and had been on edge for a few weeks. He hadn't been sleeping well. Is there something I should know? Was Simon... are you, involved in anything dubious?"

Nick and Drew looked to James in an unspoken gesture of his nomination as their spokesman. James was distinctly uncomfortable and felt ashamed that he couldn't answer Deb honestly without bringing down a major shit storm on all of them. He did his best to placate Deb, while Nick and Drew shuffled uneasily, shoe gazing, hands clasped behind their backs.

"No Deb, none of us were up to anything dodgy. We were all so excited about finding the lost cave. That's probably why Simon seemed a bit restless. We were keen to get on with exploring it before anyone else discovered it. The drug guy turning up was a tragic coincidence. Me, Nick and Drew have talked endlessly about it and we wonder if he had been watching us when we were searching the hillside."

Deb: "Sorry guys, I just find it hard to accept that such a one in a million, chance encounter has taken Simon from us."

With Deb's reply, the group fell silent as tears welled up in their eyes.

After what seemed an appropriate and respectful period of time spent commiserating and chatting outside the chapel, they moved on to Simon's favourite local pub, at which he and Deb had been irregular regulars. James, Drew and Nick found seats in a quiet corner of the lounge which had been reserved for Simon's wake. They spotted Buckie make a furtive entrance, head towards their table, only to veer away as he saw James's wife Ann join them.

James gestured to Buckie, pointing towards the only empty table across the room. Buckie hesitated, concerned that he had incurred the wrath of the three people he needed to speak to. He then ambled over to the uninviting table, close to the entrance to the toilets. James, Nick and Drew excused themselves from their table, leaving Ann to sip her wine, and wandered over to Buckie.

CHAPTER 24

The Disappearance

James, Nick and Drew sat down, joining Buckie at the pub table, their solemn expressions gradually being replaced by questioning glances. Drew and Nick flanked Buckie, James sat opposite him. Buckie felt intimidated but he was determined to see this through. With each opening of the adjacent toilet door, the stink wafting across their table caused noses to wrinkle, but the three Wednesday Club members didn't intend to linger long in Buckie's company.

James: "You're the last person we expected to see at our mate's funeral. What's this about?"

Buckie: "Sorry if you feel I've intruded, but I had to get to see you. I'm desperate and I think you are the only people that can help me."

Drew, agitated and still funerially emotional: "Don't forget the reason we know each other. You're a nasty shit who makes a living from killing anything that moves. Why the hell would we want to help you?"

Nick, sensing desperation in Buckie's tone: "Let's just hear him out Drew."

Buckie: "Thanks. My daughter Kelly has gone missing. Her mum phoned me last night. She didn't get home from school. We've been to the police, but they don't seem to have a clue where to start looking."

James: "Well despite our differences, I'm truly sorry to hear that. But what makes you think we can help?"

Buckie: "I have a feeling that Kelly's disappearance might have something to do with the drug operation that you guys very effectively destroyed. I know that Karl and Otto are dead and gone, but I wonder if they had another partner that I wasn't aware of. Maybe he blames me for what you guys did. And by the way, I won't say anything to anyone, but I put two and two together when I heard about Karl's death. What was it the police said? You guys were just innocent bystanders. Hmmm, I don't think so."

Drew's face had started to redden: "Are you trying to blackmail us? Don't forget we have you by the balls... The gun with your prints all over it. Do you remember?"

Buckie: "No, this isn't blackmail, its desperation. How could I forget the gun. But that's not important now. I don't give a shit about myself, its Kelly I'm worried about."

James: "What makes you think we could do a better job than the police?"

Buckie: "You just seem to be good at dealing with shit. You're clearly switched on, clever people not afraid to jump feet first into a tricky situation. I thought about hiring a private detective, but apart from me being skint, I guess they'd just be retired police that would be just as clueless as our local cops. You guys are thinkers and most importantly, you have an insight into this whole cannabis operation. That would give you a head start."

Drew: "Yes we got up close to the cannabis operation as you call it and look where it got us! What do you think today was all about?"

While James couldn't conceive of the possibility that he and Buckie could ever be friends, he found the thought of a missing child nightmarish and the possibility that his actions might have contributed to her disappearance was devastating. He and Deb had lovingly brought up two children, a boy and a girl, and putting himself in Buckie's shoes, James couldn't imagine anything more distressing than what he was going through.

James: "That's horrendous Buckie. Hopefully Kelly will turn up unharmed soon. I'd like to help. Give me your number and I'll mull it over and call you in the morning. How old is Kelly?"

Buckie: "She's nine. Does that mean you'll help me?"

James: "I'll call you tomorrow. Let's leave it there 'till then."

With that, Buckie left the pub, feet dragging and head held low.

Before re-joining Ann who was now sat alone at her table with an empty wine glass, James, Nick and Drew held a quick conflab about Buckie's predicament and his request for their assistance. Drew and Nick declined any involvement in Buckie's problem, for their own different reasons.

Drew knew he could never reconcile his differences with Buckie and despite feeling sad that a nine-year old girl was missing, he knew he just couldn't get involved. "She's probably run away to avoid having to see Buckie. Who would want to be around that cruel bastard?"

Nick was more sympathetic to Buckie's plight, but he'd had his fill of "way off piste" adventuring as he referred to their recent forays.

Despite not wanting to join James in the quest to find Kelly, Nick and Drew were very clear however that they wished to continue with the Wednesday Club, providing that in future, the choice of adventures reverted back to legitimate activities. Risk taking in adventure sports was one thing, but neither of them wanted to cross the line again into shady, illegal and dangerous territory.

James feigned disappointment, but secretly felt relieved that his two friends wouldn't be joining him in trying to help Buckie. While he really enjoyed Drew's and Nick's company, James was in many ways a natural loner and it was no secret that he was also a "bit of a control freak" as Ann often referred to him. If he was to have any chance of success in finding Kelly, the huge undertaking he was about to embark on needed a definite strategy, which would have to be implemented quickly and resolutely. That process would be diluted by the more democratic and debated process by which Wednesday Club activities were normally organised.

With Buckie's departure, James, Nick and Drew returned to reminiscing over the fun times they had had with Simon. They will certainly miss him. The Wednesday Club will never quite be the same again, but the three remaining members are determined to continue seeking out new ideas and activities to occupy their hyperactive minds and their unwittingly increasing addiction to adrenalin.

Even as they drank their consoling beers and mourned the loss of their friend, James's wandering mind was becoming preoccupied with thoughts of the missing Kelly. He was already planning the first stage of his search. He decided that the starting point should be to establish whether Otto and Karl did have any associates who might be set on revenge. It occurred to him that the obvious trail to follow would be the Manchester cannabis distribution network. If Otto and Karl's "genetics" were as renowned and sought as they had claimed, then a search for suppliers of the drug that went by the name of "Otto's top shit" must be a good starting point.

CHAPTER 25

Barking up The Wrong Tree

James was not a natural liar and having to deceive Ann over the past few months by smoke-screening his numerous trips, many of them nocturnal, was taking its toll on his conscience and on their relationship. He decided that he must now be open with her regarding the task he had just agreed to. He didn't share the long and tortuous route by which they had arrived at this point, as that would be a huge emotional burden for her. The starting point for his openness would simply be that an acquaintance, Buckie, was in need of help to find his missing daughter and that in desperation, he had turned to James.

The day after Simon's funeral, James called Buckie and arranged to meet him at his home. In his usual thorough method of approach to any project or activity he was responsible for, he wanted to start off armed with as much knowledge and background information as possible. His only source at this point was Buckie.

James quizzed Buckie in-depth on every detail of Kelly's life, covering her relationship with him, her mother and step-dad and many other aspects, some of which Buckie failed to understand the relevance of. They also went over the history of Buckie's reluctant collaboration with Otto and Karl in the setting up and running of their cannabis growing business.

Despite the intrusive nature of James's probing, Buckie answered all his questions with as much honesty and detail as was possible. He desperately wanted Kelly back home and safe, so he was anxious to assist James in any way he could.

James refused Buckie's offer of fee or expenses, he considered it his duty to help Kelly out of a sense of culpability; what if the actions of the Wednesday Club had triggered this situation? Also, as a concerned, caring person who was horrified at the thought of child abduction, he really wanted to help, regardless of the issue of blame. He had witnessed the destructive results of Otto's and Karl's involvement in people trafficking and was determined to prevent Kelly becoming another victim of this evil crime.

On completing his lengthy grilling of Buckie, James's final request was that Buckie should send him recent pictures of Kelly to his phone, along with an approximation of her height, weight, clothes and shoe sizes.

The preliminary information gathering stage over, James then moved on to start the hunt for Kelly. That evening, he caught the Metrolink tram into Manchester city centre and sought out the areas which were obviously frequented by drug users, and therefore drug dealers. Being his home city, James was very familiar with Manchester and it didn't take long for him to locate some likely candidates to question. His first stop was close to the colourful Arch of Chinatown, the first true imperial Chinese arch erected in Europe. James had previously noticed that the benches which surround the adjacent garden are frequently used by drug addicts, rough sleepers and drunks.

James approached two scruffy young men who sat propping each other up on one of the benches. The smaller guy's eyes were staring blankly towards the sky, while his companion appeared slightly more alert. James tried to engage in conversation with the men, opening by asking if they knew where he might get "some stuff". Neither of them answered, they didn't even make eye contact, so not wanting to waste any time, James moved on towards the next bench.

He approached seven people in the small area of the square, without success. Not one of them had uttered a word of response or even acknowledged his presence. He decided to move on towards Piccadilly Station. As he was leaving the square, a voice behind him said "you won't get any sense out of this lot mate."

James turned around to face the owner of the voice. A middle aged, unshaven but well-dressed man with long, greasy, grey hair stood uncomfortably close, his chin pushed forward in a challenging demeanour. James took a step backwards and responded; "Why not?"

The stranger replied, holding out his hand to introduce himself: "Coz they're zombied. I'm Steve by the way."

James, cautiously shook Steve's hand: "Zombied? What do you mean?"

Steve: "They're on Spice... you've heard of that haven't you? They won't be back on planet Earth for a good few hours mate. Who are you and what are you after?"

James: "I heard you can get some pretty good weed around here. Apparently, it's called Otto's top shit."

Steve: "I can't get hold of that stuff, but I can get you something just as good if you want. Cheaper too."

James: "Thanks, but I've been told to get Otto's top shit and nothing else."

Steve was quick to lose his patience: "Well take my word for it mate, you can't get that shit anymore. Top shit or not."

James: "Why not? Can you tell me who might be able to get me some?"

Steve raised his voice almost to a shout. Spit spattered from his mouth as he replied: "I've fucking told you. Are you deaf? That stuff's not around any longer. If I can't get it, then nobody can. Is that clear?"

James: "Ok, I get the message."

With that brief and terse discussion with one of Manchester's street drug distributors, James wandered off towards Piccadilly to try his luck there. He had to find a link to Otto's and Karl's network, if it still existed.

He asked the same questions in the Piccadilly area, receiving similar tetchy and negative responses. He moved on to three other likely spots he had identified, only to be told again that Otto's precious product was no longer available.

Frustrated, James made his way back home. Sitting on the late night Metrolink tram, he contemplated the implications of the dead end he had met so early on in his investigation. It could mean only one thing; that with Otto's and Karl's deaths, their illicit business and supply operation had also died. What this told James, was that he had been barking up the wrong tree. He was now almost certain that Kelly's disappearance wasn't connected with the drug operation he and his friends had inadvertently destroyed.

James had to rethink and re-plan his approach. His next phase of inquiry would lead him into a realm more sinister and evil-tinged than the one he and his friends had stumbled into in the Wednesday Club's incursion into Otto's and Karl's World.